PEPPERMINT PIXIES

WINTER WITCHES OF HOLIDAY HAVEN

DANIELLE GARRETT

BOOKS BY DANIELLE GARRETT

BEECHWOOD HARBOR MAGIC MYSTERIES

Murder's a Witch

Twice the Witch

Witch Slapped

Witch Way Home

Along Came a Ghost

Lucky Witch

Betwixt: A Beechwood Harbor Collection

One Bad Witch

A Royal Witch

First Place Witch

Sassy Witch

The Witch Is Inn

Men Love Witches

Goodbye's a Witch

BEECHWOOR HARBOR GHOST MYSTERIES

The Ghost Hunter Next Door

Ghosts Gone Wild

When Good Ghosts Get the Blues

Big Ghosts Don't Cry

Diamonds are a Ghost's Best Friend

Ghosts Just Wanna Have Fun

Bad Ghosts Club

SUGAR SHACK WITCH MYSTERIES

Sprinkles and Sea Serpents

Grimoires and Gingeread

NINE LIVES MAGIC MYSTERIES

Witchy Whiskers

Hexed Hiss-tory

HAVEN PARANORMAL ROMANCES

Once Upon a Hallow's Eve

A TOUCH OF MAGIC MYSTERIES

Cupid in a Bottle

Newly Wed and Slightly Dead

Couture and Curses

Wedding Bells and Deadly Spells

S ummertime in the North Pole sounds like something of an oxymoron, but as the quaint little town of Holiday Haven approached the summer solstice, there was a slight shift in the air. The busyness of Christmas time was about to begin and the residents, myself included, were enjoying the last few slow-moving weeks before life kicked back into high gear. Of course, at the North Star Reindeer Sanctuary things never slowed down too much. Hotels and inns in Holiday Haven often ran specials to attract off-season tourists to the greater North Pole, and we still opened our sanctuary to guests two times a week during the summer months. It kept us busy, but was a welcome reprieve from the fire-hose stream of guests we hosted in the winter. And even though we didn't have tourists on the property daily, we still had our herd of reindeer to tend to, and farm chores don't stop for anything.

I didn't mind it though. At nearly thirty-three years old, this way of life was all I knew. I'd never traveled outside the North Pole before and could go weeks without needing to leave my family's property to run into town for supplies or other errands.

Well, that last part was quickly changing. I smiled across the frozen, snow-covered field as a white, winged horse swooped down from the clouds to land on the stone driveway beside the old farmhouse where my parents lived. A man in a black parka and snow pants dismounted the horse with a fluid grace that spoke to the years of experience he had riding the stunning creature named Ullr.

"Looks like it's time for me to go," I told my reindeer, Starlea, stroking my hand over the thick snow-white hair covering her chest. My fingers snagged on a small braid and I sighed. My little cousins had visited the week before and insisted on treating her like a live-action My Little Pony doll. Luckily, Starlea didn't mind the attention and let the girls play "pony" beauty parlor. It had taken hours to brush away the layer of glitter hairspray they'd used on her back when I wasn't looking. "I'll have to brush that out when I get back," I told her. "I thought I got them all."

"Lumi!" the man called, already heading down the driveway. He smiled at me and sent my heart tumbling in a somersault. Nearly six months had passed since our first official date, an evening spent at the annual Yule Ball, but somehow I still got that butterfly feeling in my stomach every time I saw him.

With one final pat to Starlea's shoulder, I hurried for the wooden fence partitioning off the field from the long, winding driveway. "Hi! How was your flight? Seems like a nice day for it." I glanced up at the patches of blue sky peeking between fluffy white clouds.

Corbin Frost, the prince of the Frost Kingdom, nodded. "The perfect day for flying. Although, I must say, things are looking even better down here on the ground." With a sly smile he reached over the fence to cup the side of my face, his dark brown eyes sparkling before he moved his lips to mine.

"Lumi!"

I jerked back from the kiss and turned to find my familiar, Sugarplum, an Arctic hare, hopping toward us. The hare's brown pelt stood out starkly against the snow packed along the driveway. "What's going on, Sugarplum?"

"That man is back," the hare replied, giving Corbin a sideways glance. "Hello, Prince Corbin."

"Hello, Sugarplum," Corbin said with a chuckle. "You don't have to call me *prince*, remember?"

I glared up the driveway. From where we stood, the front porch of the house wasn't visible but I already knew who Sugarplum was talking about. "He has some nerve," I growled under my breath.

"Who?" Corbin asked.

I hauled myself over the split-rail fence. "Percy Lowell. He's a real estate developer from New York. He's been snatching up property all over the North Pole and surrounding areas, including Holiday Haven, so he can build short-term rentals and hotels. He's been after my parents for months now, trying to get them to agree to sell off some of the sanctuary's acreage. He's cagey about his precise plans, but it's pretty obvious what his goal is.

The North Pole and the smaller communities are filling up fast. There is only so much inhabitable land, which is driving prices through the roof."

Corbin frowned. "I can't imagine your parents ever going along with something like that."

"No. Of course not." I shook my head. "But Mr. Lowell doesn't seem to like the word *no*."

"Last time he was here, Stephen had to threaten to call the Holiday Haven police to get him off the property!" Sugarplum told Corbin before he began hopping back up the driveway toward the house.

Corbin glanced over at me. "You want me to get rid of him? For good?" He paused, then cracked a grin. "Okay, that sounded way more mob boss than I intended, but you know what I mean."

I laughed. "You can give it a try, *Don* Frost."

Corbin chuckled and grabbed ahold of my hand as we began following Sugarplum. "If nothing else, I could post a couple of royal guards here at the sanctuary. Since Jack is off on his royal PR tour, they haven't got much to do anyway."

"How is that going? I'm surprised you aren't with him, to be honest. Aren't you worried about him getting himself into trouble?"

"Always," Corbin replied with a dry laugh. "But we agreed that I should stay behind to be with our father. Jack took a contingent of guards and advisors with him— ones that I picked out—and so far it seems to be going well."

I squeezed Corbin's hand a little tighter. "How is your dad? Any improvement?"

Corbin shook his head. His jaw flexed but he didn't speak.

Jack Frost had been crowned king right before the Yule Ball, taking over for their father as he'd fallen terminally ill. Jack wasn't anyone's first pick for taking the throne, not even his own, but there was a line of succession and centuries of royal tradition to uphold. Corbin was eighteen months younger than Jack, and while he had no interest in taking the crown for himself, most in the Frost Kingdom would agree that he would make for a better king. Selfishly, I was very glad he was not. It was odd enough dating a full-fledged prince. I wasn't sure things would have turned out the way they had if he'd been crowned over Jack.

My mother stood on the porch of the farmhouse, her sherpa-lined slippers anchored to the welcome mat. From the look in her eyes she wasn't too happy about being pulled from her work. Percy Lowell was dressed sharply, as always, like something of a caricature from movies set in New York. A tailored pinstripe suit, tie and pocket square, expensive watch, flashy car. Way too much cologne.

"... a few minutes of your time. I think you'll be pleased with this new offer. It involves a much smaller parcel of land, but an even bigger sale price," Percy was saying, his obviously over-whitened teeth gleaming.

"Mr. Lowell," my mom said, her tone taking on the *don't mess with me* pitch I recognized from my teen years, "as we have continually told you, we are not—nor will we *ever* be—interested in selling even a single square foot of our land to you or anyone else."

I approached the side of the porch. "Mom?"

She glanced over at me, her expression pinched. It relaxed slightly when she lifted her gaze and saw Corbin at my side. "Corbin. I didn't realize you were coming today." A smile quirked at the corners of her lips as she shifted her attention back to Percy Lowell. "Mr. Lowell, I realize you're from New York, but even you must know who Prince Corbin Frost is, right?"

Percy's thick but manicured brows jumped up his preternaturally smooth forehead as he turned to face us. "Prince? I mean, um, well, it's an honor," he quickly corrected as he scurried forward to extend a hand over the banister.

"Is there a reason you're harassing Mrs. Northrop and the rest of her family?" Corbin asked, not accepting the man's hand.

"Harassing?" Percy gave a titter of nervous laughter. "I think that's a bit strong, don't you, Diana?"

My mom crossed her arms.

"I see." Percy pressed his thin lips together and gave a short nod. "Well, let me just leave this paperwork with you and I'll leave you to the rest of your day."

He held out a black portfolio toward my mother, who kept her arms crossed, her expression unflinching. With a barely contained snort of derision, Percy settled for leaving the packet on the wide plank railing, then scampered down the handful of steps, back to his shiny black luxury car parked beside my dad's beat-up farm truck.

He offered a curt wave as he backed his car up.

"That's the first sensible thing that man's done since he darkened our doorstep," Mom said, scoffing as she watched Percy's taillights retreat down the sloped drive. "Thank you, Corbin."

Corbin held up a hand. "No thanks required."

She smiled at me. To say my mom was pleased about my burgeoning relationship was like saying Santa enjoyed an occasional sugar cookie.

"Would you like to come inside for some lemonade?" she asked. "It's made fresh. The market got a huge shipment of lemons last week. I had to wrestle a bag away from that harpy, Julia Quip, but it serves her right."

I resisted the urge to slap one hand across my face.

Corbin chuckled. "Sounds like there's a story there."

"Please don't ask," I begged.

Sugarplum scampered up the front porch and my mom opened the door to let him inside once he thumped his hind legs against the porch a few times to knock off the excess snow. "I'm not much for lemonade, but if there's still some of that carrot cake I wouldn't say no."

Mom headed in after Sugarplum, then Corbin and I followed after stomping off our own boots. Life on a farm didn't lend itself to having a spotless house, but my mom did her best to keep up with the constant stream of muck. As a rule, all boots had to come off upon entering the house. Corbin was used to it by now. We both removed our boots and set them on the wooden rack beside the front door before proceeding through the living room and dining room into the kitchen.

I went to the fridge and got the glass pitcher of fresh-squeezed lemonade while Mom got glasses down from the cupboard. "Oh, Corbin, dear, you go take a seat.

You've had a long trek. We'll bring this out. Are you hungry?"

Sugarplum and I exchanged a look behind her back.

Corbin smiled politely. "I'm all right. Thank you, Mrs. Northrop."

"Oh, please, I've told you to call me Diana." She turned and busied herself with preparing a tray of snacks in spite of his reply. Sugarplum hopped around her feet, hoping for a piece of carrot cake—his favorite—to come down from above. He was an expert at dodging out of her way before she had the chance to trip over him, but even still, she paused and nudged him gently in the side. "Wait your turn, Sugarplum."

Sulking, he hopped across the kitchen to the basket in the corner my mom kept for him. He turned in three circles and lay down, his ears flattening behind his head.

Corbin was still standing halfway between the kitchen and dining room and I gave him a little shooing motion before my mom could. Grinning, he turned and went back into the living room. The front door opened and my dad appeared, still in the process of knocking a layer of snow off his boots. When he glanced up, he did a double take and then wound up doing an awkward bow mid-stomp. "Prince Corbin, hello."

Corbin held out a hand. "Nice to see you, Mr. Northrop."

"Oh, Jim please," my dad replied, gratefully shaking his hand.

"You guys have got to relax when he's around," I whispered to my mom. "He doesn't like special treatment."

"It's not special treatment, Lumi. It's just our way of

showing respect," she argued. "Does he like carrot cake? We have enough here?"

Sugarplum perked up as Mom grabbed a plastic container from the fridge and carved out a two-by-two-inch square of frosted carrot cake. She scraped off most of the frosting with a butter knife—which sent his ears back to flat against his head.

I glanced at the tray she'd already loaded down with smoked meats, crackers, cheese, spears of pickle, and a segmented box of various nuts. "I think we're all set. The only reason we came over here was to help get rid of Percy, not for a three-course meal." I exhaled. There was no use in trying to fight her on it.

Mom paused to take a sip of her lemonade. "Well, it's a good thing you showed up. Otherwise, you and your dad might be heading to the police station in hopes of bailing me out of the pokey."

I smiled into my own glass of lemonade. It was a rare summertime treat, and somehow managed to sound good even though it was only slightly warmer than usual outside.

"He certainly knows how to get things done, doesn't he?" Mom continued.

I looked through the archway where Corbin was speaking with my dad. "His grumpy side does come in handy from time to time," I said with a soft giggle. When we'd first met, I couldn't imagine ever willingly spending time with the man. He'd been irritable, bossy, even accusatory. However, in hindsight, I could appreciate that he was worried sick about his brother, as well as his own future, because if we hadn't managed to track down Jack,

Corbin himself would have been forced to take the crown in his place.

He'd relaxed considerably since then, but he was still used to running a palace full of staff and guards, not to mention wrangling his brother, who had a reputation for all manner of vices.

After depositing Sugarplum's snack into the small silver bowl beside the basket, Mom grabbed the tray of refreshments, leaving me to carry the drinks out on a second tray.

"Where are you two headed today?" Mom asked Corbin as we entered the living room. She set her tray down on the coffee table and then turned to grab a glass of lemonade from my tray. She handed it to Corbin with a smile and then went to her favorite chair placed opposite the sofa where he sat. "Off to see the construction of the beach bubble? I heard it's going to be quite a sight this year! Mrs. Claus herself is said to be involved in the preparations."

I blinked. "Really? Wow."

"This will be my first year attending one of the Pole's summer celebrations," Corbin said, reaching over to snag a square of the carrot cake.

Sugarplum would approve of his taste, at least.

"Oh, you're going to love it!" Mom exclaimed, nearly sloshing her lemonade. "They cast a charm in a huge area and make it feel like a warm summer day, with palm trees and a swimming pool that looks like the ocean, with waves and everything. There's a tiki bar with all sorts of tropical drinks. Rumor has it they've even brought in some mermaids and mermen to serve as the lifeguards."

Corbin looked impressed. "I guess Lumi was right, it sounds like I need to go shopping for something to wear."

"The frost pixies have been selected to perform a special dance for everyone," Mom continued. "They've been very secretive about it so far, but I'm sure whatever they come up with will be wonderful."

"A little fire and ice flavor, huh?" Corbin joked.

Mom opened her mouth to reply when a loud *bang* suddenly shook the front door. My dad jumped to his feet and went to peer out the window.

"What was that, Jim?" Mom asked, craning around in her chair.

Without replying, my dad opened the door and revealed a broken-apart mound of snow on the welcome mat. He frowned down at it. "A ... snowball, I think." He stepped out onto the porch but returned a moment later shaking his head as he closed the door. "I don't know who threw it. Maybe a neighbor kid playing a prank."

The sanctuary didn't *have* neighbors. At least, not in the typical sense. There were other homes on patches of land nearby, but the closest had to be over half a mile away. It was a long trek for a couple of bored kids to make just to throw a few snowballs around.

Dad retook his seat and we moved on.

Corbin glanced at me, then said, "We should probably be on our way soon. Lumi's agreed to take me around Holiday Haven to look at some potential venues for Jack's last stop on his publicity tour. We had booked the town hall but there was a mix-up and the other reservation was made first, so we pulled out."

"Why not have it here at the sanctuary?" Mom suggested.

"We're not really set up for something like that, are we?" I asked. "Last time we hosted the Frost King, we had months of lead time."

Mom flapped her hand. "That was in the middle of the Christmas season. Things are always more complicated that time of year. My work schedule is light right now, so I could be at your disposal, Prince Corbin. Think of me as your personal full-time event coordinator. Wouldn't that be something?"

Corbin looked at me. "What do you think, Lumi?"

I swallowed. "I ... I guess so."

"Then it's settled!" Mom set her lemonade on the table and clasped her hands together. "After we finish here, we can go out to the main barn and see what we can come up with. I promise, with some elbow grease, we can transform it into something really special. You won't even be able to tell a pack of stinky reindeer live in there."

Yeah, sure, just a touch of elbow grease and a bucket full of magic.

2

"*W*hat are you envisioning for the event, Pri —I mean, Corbin?" Mom asked as we strolled down the driveway toward the gate that led into the field encircling the main barn. "Are you thinking something seasonal, in line with the summer solstice? Or would you prefer something wintry?"

"To tell you the truth, Diana, I'm not usually very hands-on for the planning," Corbin replied with a polite smile. "The only reason I came out to scout for venues in Holiday Haven was because it gave me a reason to get out of the castle and come see Lumi."

I smiled as I unlinked my arm from Corbin's and went ahead to open the gate. "You didn't tell me that."

Mom gave me a knowing look as she passed through the gate. "I understand completely," she said. "The things we do for love. I became some kind of farmer's wife, you're turning into a party planner."

I kept my smile in place but the casual throwing around of the L-word sent my heart racing. Corbin and I hadn't said those three little words to one another, and while there had been moments they'd almost slipped from my lips, I'd held back. I wasn't sure why, exactly. Maybe it was old-fashioned, but there was a part of me that wanted him to take the lead. Or maybe deep down I was afraid he didn't feel the same way I did.

I put a little space between us and went ahead to open the barn doors. As soon as I did, a snowball shot down from the rafters and pelted Corbin in the side of the head as he came to stand beside me. He clapped a hand to his cheek. "What the—"

A second snowball flew down and I dodged just in time to avoid the same fate.

"Ugh," Mom exclaimed, "it's those pixies. They get so bored in the summer."

I frowned. Sure, the frost pixies could be a bit of a handful, and they loved a prank from time to time, but I couldn't recall a time they intentionally beaned someone. Their pranks were silly, not mean-spirited.

"Shouldn't you be practicing your dance number for the solstice celebration?" Mom called up at the rafters.

A wild peal of tiny giggles sounded and a pair of silver-winged pixies dove at us, sending a spray of ammunition in rapid fire. Only this time they weren't hurling tiny snowballs at us. Instead, we were bombarded by individually wrapped peppermint candy canes, each one barely thicker than a toothpick. Before I could fully register what was happening, a fight broke out between a pair of pixies hovering over one of the reindeer stalls.

"Knock it off, Astrid!" Dewdrop, the one on the left,

screeched as Astrid, one of the larger pixies, tugged at her wings.

With her teeth.

"Are they at it again?" Sugarplum asked with a disgusted scoff as he hopped into the barn. "They've been like this all morning."

"Astrid! Dewdrop! Stop that at once!" I shouted, striding toward them. "What is the meaning of all this?"

Neither of the pixies listened. Dewdrop managed to use some momentum and tumbled Astrid overhead, still suspended in the air, before wrapping her in a headlock.

"Oh, for Rudolph's sake," I muttered.

On the other side of the aisleway, three other pixies popped up and sent another round of mini candy canes raining down. "Stop that!" I growled.

"My guess is they've had way too many of these things," Sugarplum said, thumping one of his back feet at a candy cane lying on the cement floor beside him. "Sugar high. You know how they get."

He had a point. Every year at Christmas time we had a hot cocoa stand and often had to tell Arabella, the fairy who ran it, to cut the pixies off before they got carried away. But I'd never seen them turn violent on a sugar high. At their worst, they'd just over-frost the wreaths and Christmas trees with their snowflake pixie dust or start chatting the guests' ears off at a million-words-per-minute pace.

Astrid broke loose of the headlock and punched Dewdrop in the face. Dewdrop let out a savage cry and dove for Astrid's legs. She managed to catch Astrid off-guard and they both slammed into the wooden half-wall separating the stall from the one beside it.

"Enough!" I shouted.

Giggles sounded from over my shoulder and I whipped around just in time to see the three pixies fly toward me. One of them, Pinecone, grabbed my braided hair and tugged hard. "Ouch! Hey, cut that out."

Another pixie, Frosty, pulled at the back of my collar and sent a shower of snow down my back. The third, Noelle, cackled maniacally and licked a candy cane before sticking it to my cheek.

"Knock it off!" I screamed, flailing at the three taunting pixies.

A blast of wind rolled through the barn, strong enough that it nearly knocked me off my feet. My three tiny assailants went tumbling through the air and hit the stack of hay bales at the far end of the barn.

I straightened and gave Corbin a grateful look before closing in on the pixies, still dazed as they lay in the stray bits of straw scattered around the bales. "I don't know what's gotten into them."

"Hey!" Astrid cried out, poking her head over the stall. "You can't do that!"

Dewdrop popped up beside her, one tiny fist shaking. "This is war, humans!"

"Astrid, Dewdrop, what are you two fighting about?"

Dewdrop soared down and grabbed a handful of reindeer poop. "Don't make me use this!"

Behind me, my mom shrieked. "That's it, I'm going to get your father. This is a brand-new cashmere sweater!"

Corbin came to stand beside me. "What's going on

with them?" he asked. "Are they really just on a sugar high?"

"I—I don't know," I stammered. "I've never seen them like this before."

"Don't talk about us like we're not standing right here!" Dewdrop demanded, bringing one hand back like she was about to throw out the first pitch at the World Series.

I conjured a wall of ice, blocking the pellets before they could hit Corbin and me. Using the cover of the temporary shield, I ran to the corner of the barn and grabbed my wooden staff. Across the barn, the three in the hay pile were getting back to their feet, and judging by their tiny clenched fists, they were none too happy with Corbin's blast of north wind.

I sent a surge of magic from my hand into the ancient staff. Runes carved into the wood burst to life with glowing blue light. "I don't want to do this," I warned the pixies, holding up the staff, "but if you don't calm down, I'll have no choice."

The ice wall was clear enough that the pixies could see the illuminated runes. Astrid and Dewdrop screamed and flew at the ice barrier. With a flick of my wrist, I sent another layer of ice to reinforce and extend the first wall. Panic started to build in my chest. My threat had been somewhat empty. The staff contained all manner of magic, but I generally used it only to summon the pixies from the woods when they overslept or in case of emergency. And right now, the idea of summoning the rest of the pixies seemed like a bad idea, considering that whatever was causing this sudden morph in personality might have run through the entire pixie colony.

The sanctuary was surrounded by acres of frozen forest land. The frost pixies lived deep in the woods and while they enjoyed their work on the farm, they still spent the majority of their time isolated, amongst the other pixies and creatures of the wild. Not all of the pixies came to work on the sanctuary. There were countless scores of the pixies in the woods. And if all of them had turned wild … well, there was no telling how much damage they might cause.

Wincing, I decided I had to try something. I barked out a spell and slammed the end of my staff against the concrete floor. A peal of ancient magic boomed through the barn. The pixies dove toward the ground and I seized upon their distraction, conjuring a dome of ice to surround them like a giant snow globe. When the pixies realized what I'd done, they hissed and shook their fists at me.

"I don't know how long that will hold," I said, giving the dome a nervous glance. Inside, the pixies had begun beating against the ice, but their small bodies weren't strong enough to break through. However, if they calmed down long enough to try working together, it was possible they might find a way, especially once the ice started to melt. The reindeer barn wasn't as warm as inside my parents' house or the interior of my cottage on the back acreage, but it was kept above freezing and unless I froze a new layer of ice on the dome every hour or two, eventually it would melt away.

There was also the chance the pixies would get

increasingly frustrated and start turning on each other. I didn't want anyone to get hurt, but I also didn't think I'd be able to work quickly enough to trap them all individually.

We needed to get to the bottom of this, and fast.

Turning back to Corbin, I set my jaw. "We have to go see Doc Patches."

DOC PATCHES, the lead veterinarian in the North Pole, was personally on call to help Santa any time, day or night. I had no idea how old the elf was, but rumor had it he'd been one of Santa's lifelong friends, and Santa was very, *very* old.

He came to Holiday Haven on a regular basis to check on Santa's retired herd, and I'd known him since before I could walk. The lanky elf was warm and friendly, but became precise and analytical while working. It was impressive that he managed to stay so sharp, considering his advanced years.

I rode on Starlea's back while Corbin took to the sky on Ullr, and we flew to the North Pole to visit Doc Patches at his clinic, which was only a quick snowmobile's ride from Santa's compound on the hill. His clinic had the same gingerbread charm as the rest of the businesses on the cobblestone street, a fresh layer of snow covering the pitched roof. Two young kids stood in front of the toy shop next door, talking excitedly as they watched a magical flying train set cruise around the shop's display window. One of them looked over his shoulder as we made our descent, and his eyes went wide. He tugged at his friend's jacket sleeve and both of them practically tripped over themselves to come and watch Ullr and Starlea touch down.

"Wow, mister, I like your horse!" the first boy said, grinning from ear to ear.

Corbin chuckled as he dismounted and began walking Ullr to the red and white striped hitching post out in front of Doc Patches' clinic. "You think you could keep him company for a little bit?" He reached into his coat as both boys jumped up and down and promised to take good care of him. With a smile, Corbin thanked them and handed each boy a pair of rolled oat balls. "These are his favorite," he explained.

We laced the reins to the post and left the two boys to dote on the pair of animals while we stepped inside Patches' clinic.

The inside of the clinic was just as cutesy as the exterior, with twinkling lights and a large, decorated Christmas tree in the corner, its ornaments all animal themed. The desk in the center of the lobby was shaped like a sleigh and a bespectacled female elf sat behind it, a headset perched on her head of silvery-white locks. "Good afternoon, Mrs. Patches," I said with a warm smile.

"Lumi, dear, you're looking well!" Mrs. Patches hopped down from her stool behind the desk and bustled around to wrap me in an embrace. She stood barely higher than my waist, so I bent forward to return the warm greeting.

"Thank you. It's good to see you, too." I straightened to

my full height again and gestured toward Corbin. "This is my boyfriend, Cor—"

"Well, of course I know who he is!" Mrs. Patches interrupted, adding a little curtsey as she turned toward him. "It's a pleasure to meet you, Prince Corbin."

"Likewise," he replied.

Suddenly, Mrs. Patches twisted back to me, her eyes wide behind her spectacles. "Did you say *boyfriend*, dear?"

I laughed softly. "That's right."

"Oh my! I'd heard a rumor some time ago, after the Yule Ball, I believe, but you know me, I don't put much stock in the scuttlebutt around town."

I grinned. Everyone knew Mrs. Patches was an integral part of the gossip grapevine in the Pole and beyond.

"Now," Mrs. Patches said, going back around the desk, "what brings you by today? I don't see you listed in the appointment diary. Did Hazel forget to make a note? She's been extra forgetful lately, poor dear. You know, she's got a newborn at home, so I blame the lack of sleep. I remember those days like they were yesterday. Of course, they were many *many* moons ago," she added with a twinkle of laughter.

"I actually don't have an appointment," I told her. "But if there is any chance Doc has a few minutes, I really need his help with something."

"Oh, for you, he will make time!" Mrs. Patches held up one finger. "You wait right here, dear. I'll go and get him for you."

"Thank you."

She bustled down the short hallway and made a right turn, which I knew was the direction of the doctor's private office space. A few moments later both Mrs. and Dr. Patches appeared. They were something of a mismatched pair. Doc Patches was tall and lanky, while his wife was petite and plump. His hand rested on his wife's shoulder as he smiled warmly at Corbin and me from over the half-moon spectacles perched on his slightly crooked nose. The lenses magnified a pair of sparkling blue eyes that seemed to defy his advanced years with their clarity and brilliance. He wore a knit cap over the silvery-white locks that fell to his shoulders. The cap was likely made by his wife, an avid crocheter.

"Lumi Northrop *and* Prince Corbin," he exclaimed, leaving his wife's side to amble over to us. A round of handshakes and greetings were exchanged before he called us back to his exam room.

"Now, what seems to be the trouble?" he asked as he closed the door behind us. In contrast to the cozy lobby, the exam room was all business—soft blue walls and minimal decor, with a stainless-steel table and washing station dominating most of the space.

Corbin and I exchanged a glance before I spoke. "This is likely going to be an odd request, but is there any chance you have an idea as to what might cause a sudden personality shift in a frost pixie?"

Doc Patches listened patiently as I gave a quick summary of the events back at the barn. When I finished, Doc Patches frowned. "And you have no idea what preceded this encounter?"

I shook my head. "Not a clue."

"Hmm. Very strange indeed." Doc Patches ran two spindly fingers over his pointed chin. "To tell you the truth, pixies don't typically fall under my area of expertise. They're somewhere between human medicine and veterinary care. Though I'm not sure a human doctor would be of much help, either."

I nodded. "I understand. I just wasn't sure who to turn to."

Doc Patches considered the matter for another long moment, then circled his gaze back to mine. "Any other day, I would offer to come out to the sanctuary, but I'm afraid Santa Claus needs me up at the stables," he paused to glance at his watch, "here in an hour or so. The team needs their monthly checkups. It won't be too long before they start preparing for this year's run and as you know, they all need to be in tip-top shape."

"Of course."

"Could you bring one of the pixies here to the clinic instead? I should be back before suppertime and don't mind keeping the light on for you."

"If I can catch one," I replied, giving Corbin a nervous glance.

Doc Patches chuckled. "Believe me, I know from experience our winged friends are the hardest to corral for veterinary care. See what you can do. Phone Maura if you run into too much trouble and I'll see about coming directly to the sanctuary following the appointment with the big man."

Corbin placed an arm around my shoulders. "Thanks, Doc. We'll do our best."

3

*W*e left the veterinary clinic and found the two boys keeping dutiful watch over Ullr and Starlea—both of whom were nosing at the children's coats in hopes of finding more snacks. "Hey, hey," Corbin said firmly as he moved Ullr's head away, though he couldn't help smiling at his steed. "That's enough of that."

The boys laughed. "His nose tickles!"

"Thank you for watching out for them," I told them.

They exchanged a glance, then the taller one elbowed his friend. The shorter one cleared his throat and gave us a furtive glance. "Do you think we could go for a ride with you sometime?"

Corbin smiled. "We're a little short on time this afternoon, but if you come to the reindeer sanctuary on the weekends they have flying reindeer you can ride on."

"Really?" Their eyes went round as sugar cookies. "We'll be there!"

At the corner of the street, a pair of women came into

view and called the boys' names. Both of them scampered off, bursting with the news.

"I'm guessing Ullr isn't too big on the idea of pony rides even if we weren't busy," I said with a laugh as I untied Starlea's reins from the hitching post.

Corbin stroked the side of his horse's face. "Not really. He barely puts up with me most days."

Ullr huffed through his nose, sending a puff of white cloud into the air. We laughed and mounted up, ready to fly back to the sanctuary. As we approached Holiday Haven, I noticed a crowd gathered around the open-air skating rink in the center of town. I squinted, trying to figure out what had everyone's attention, but didn't see anyone on the ice until I urged Starlea to fly a little closer to the ground. A band of fairies was dancing out on the rink, sending sprays of silver and gold pixie dust over the ice, making designs with their graceful movements.

We whizzed past, momentarily drawing some of the crowd's attention, and I craned around to see more than a few people pointing up at us as we flew by. Until my relationship with Corbin began, I was well known around town, but my reputation was being "the quiet reindeer girl" or "the Northrops' daughter." Now, I was Prince Corbin's girlfriend, and that was a very different kind of attention.

The Frost Family technically had no sovereignty over the North Pole or any of the surrounding communities, but there were so-called "royal watchers" similar to those in the United States being fascinated by the British royal family. Jack Frost was often found splashed across the covers of tabloids, and whenever he was in town, a crowd tended to follow him around. Corbin kept a much lower profile. He didn't give interviews or sit for photo shoots. He wasn't the face of the Frost family, but he wasn't completely removed from the hubbub either. And currently, with Jack Frost busy performing his royal duties, and *mostly* staying out of trouble, the fascination and gossip had shifted to the romance between Corbin and the reclusive farm girl.

Or, at least, that's how the papers tend to describe me.

The past six months had been something of a crash course in being a public persona, and I still wasn't quite used to it. Attending the Yule Ball as Corbin's date had been something like crossing a bridge and then taking a match to it. There was no going back to the way things used to be, back before I'd met him. It was an odd paradox, how my life had changed forever but somehow still felt the same. Most days, I went through my familiar routine. I worked around the sanctuary, caring for the animals and helping to run the family's business. For long stretches, it would feel normal. Then I'd go into town for one thing or another, and see people gathering to whisper in little pockets as I passed them on the street. Some people were brazen enough to approach me and attempt to dig into my love life. Others took my photo without my permission. When Corbin and I were together, people were more polite, but we still wound up having candid photos published in the tabloids.

Corbin was worth the extra attention, of course, but I did find myself less willing to go into town these days, preferring to visit Corbin at his home in the Frost Kingdom. People there were used to him wandering the streets and frequenting the local shops and restaurants. And if things got hairy, there were royal guards who could step in and provide space for us to escape from the prying eyes.

I tried not to get ahead of myself, but my daily life left too much silence, and my thoughts often wandered. Lately, they'd been wondering what might happen if things were to become more serious between me and the Frost Prince. Our lives could hardly be more opposite one another, and I wasn't sure how we would ever manage to find a way to blend them together. Before Corbin came along, I figured I would stay on my family's property long term. Maybe forever. I didn't like to think about it, but my parents weren't getting any younger, and one day they would need someone to step up and run the place. My older brother, Stephen, had two young children who split their time between living with him and their mother, Stephen's ex-wife, in the North Pole. I knew it put a lot of strain on him not being able to see his kids every day, and wondered if one day he would leave and move to the Pole permanently. Our younger brother, Klein, already lived in the North Pole and worked as a banker. He had no interest in reindeer or running a farm.

That left me. The sanctuary was my entire life. It was in my blood. My magic itself was intrinsically tied to the land.

But then Corbin's life and blood were equally inter-twined with his royal duties. It would be just as compli-cated for him to leave his life in the Frost Kingdom to come and live in Holiday Haven as it would be for me to leave home and move there.

Despite my best efforts to slow down and enjoy our time together, I couldn't help but feel that maybe we were kidding ourselves even trying to make things work between us long-term.

Up ahead, Ullr suddenly banked to the right, snapping my attention from my wandering thoughts. He flew in a wide half-circle, back the way we'd come, and I pulled Starlea's reins and guided her to follow, though I wasn't sure what had caught Corbin's eye. It took a second, but then I saw it. There, in the snow below, a set of tracks shot out away from the town, and in their wake were a series of frozen ice sculptures formed into half-pipes, ramps, and even one full loop-de-loop.

Jack.

Corbin urged Ullr on faster, and the large horse's wings beat furiously as the pair swooped down low to the ground and followed the tracks. I nudged Starlea with my heels and we zoomed a little faster. She didn't have the benefit of wings, but her magic was strong, and we could almost keep pace with the horse ahead.

We followed the tracks in the snow—a telltale sign of Jack's favorite snowmobile—until we caught up to him out in the tundra surrounding Holiday Haven. Corbin took Ullr higher, in an arc over the snowmobile, and then swung around to fly at Jack head on.

Jack let loose a loud *whoop* as the brothers locked into a dangerous game of chicken. Corbin and Ullr pulled away from the collision course first, just in time for Jack to cast some of his magic ahead. Out of thin air, a ramp made entirely out of ice appeared and he drove the snow-mobile up it at full blast, suspending in the air for a full moment, sunlight gleaming off the pair of frost-wyverns painted along the sides, before he landed with another loud holler of excitement.

Shaking my head, I landed Starlea at the base of the newly constructed ramp and dismounted. Jack peeled a donut in the snow, sending a spray of ice out in an arc, before coming to a stop. His tawny hair was tousled and every bit as wild as the grin spread across his handsome face. There was no doubt the pair were brothers, even though Corbin's hair was as dark as Jack's was light. Their faces were both chiseled, though in slightly different ways. Corbin's jaw was stronger, harsher, and while he had an excellent smile, it seemed that whenever he was around his brother, he took on a dark and broody expression that stood in stark contrast to his older brother's jovial disposition.

"Brother!" Jack bellowed, tossing his arms overhead.

Ullr offered an inpatient snort as his rider dismounted. "What do you think you're doing out here?" Corbin demanded, stalking through the snow to get to his brother.

"What does it look like I'm doing?" Jack replied, gesturing around himself. "Blowing off a little steam. You should try it sometime, Corby."

Jack slid a smirk past his brother toward me. "You know, I really thought you'd bring out his fun side."

I sighed. "It's nice to see you, too, Jack."

Jack laughed and slung one leg over his snowmobile, leaving the engine idling. "What brings you two out here, anyway? Were you sneaking away for a romantic tryst? If

29

so, say no more, I'll saddle up and blast out of here lick-ety-split."

Corbin clapped a hand on his brother's shoulder. "You're not going anywhere."

Jack's eyes still sparkled with mirth even as he groaned and feigned an exasperated sigh. "If you needed a wingman just say so. I'll talk you up." Peeking back at me, he winked. "Did old Corby here ever tell you the story about the time he single-handedly saved a whole nest of baby wood sprites after a servant found them in one of the castle's guest rooms? He's an old softy, I tell you. Very sensitive. In touch with his feelings."

"Shut. Up," Corbin ground out through clenched teeth.

"What?" Jack protested. "Chicks like stories about animals."

Corbin was undeterred. "You're supposed to be on Moonstone Island doing a press tour, not out here popping wheelies in the snow!"

"Technically speaking, dear brother, one can't do *wheelies* on a snowmobile."

Corbin's jaw flexed.

Jack laughed. "Relax, my little prickled pear. The PR thing was a slam dunk. I had all of those stuffy ambassadors eating out of the palm of my hand. One of them even slipped me her number after the Q&A." Jack waggled his brows. "What do you think of that? Is a king allowed to date an ambassador to a foreign island? She did have a very nice—"

"Jack!" Corbin growled. "There was supposed to be a dinner following the event."

"Oh, right, well the head guy, Lord Prattles-on-for-days wasn't feeling well and asked if we could reschedule, which I, being the gracious and humble king that I am, agreed to." Jack slapped a hand on Corbin's chest. "So, brother, that means you have nothing to worry your pretty little head over."

He moved past Corbin and sauntered over to me. He draped an arm around my shoulders and leaned in with a conspiratorial whisper, "Seriously, Lumi, tell me just what it is you see in this guy! He's always such a wet blanket. You want to go for a spin? I promise you a good time. With your magic and mine working together, just think of the course we could build! I'll bet we could manage a double loop. What do you say?"

I laughed even as I rolled my eyes. "Do we have to have this conversation every time we see one another?" I asked.

"Hey, you can't blame a guy for trying," Jack said. "How's life on the horse farm?"

"Reindeer sanctuary," I corrected.

"Right, right." Jack dropped his arm and wandered back to his snowmobile, not waiting for my answer. Jack wasn't generally interested in much of anything that didn't directly relate to him. I wasn't sure how any woman managed to put up with his endless chatter about himself, but then, considering the personality of his last girlfriend, they probably spent their dates competing to see which one could talk about themselves the most before the dessert course.

"Where are your guards?" Corbin asked. "I specifically told them not to let you out of their sight."

Jack laughed. "Don't worry, Corby, they're all probably three ales deep at the pub by now. I told them to put it on

31

the royal tab. It's not like I need them out here. What's the worst that could happen?"

"You know, for someone who got kidnapped and nearly killed six months ago, you'd think you wouldn't ask questions like that," Corbin muttered. He dragged a hand over his jaw.

"Hey, I'm still here, aren't I?" Jack asked with a laugh.

Corbin groaned. "And where are you going now?" he asked as Jack climbed back on his snowmobile and revved the engine. "You're meeting with the council tomorrow afternoon, aren't you?"

"Yeah, yeah. I'm crashing at the chalet tonight, *with* the guards, before you even ask. We'll all go back to the castle in the morning."

Corbin hesitated, as though looking for a hole in the plan, but when he couldn't find one, he gave a slight nod. "All right."

Jack gestured at the untouched land ahead of him. "It doesn't have quite the same thrill as racing down the streets of Holiday Haven, but it will do."

Technically, he was following the rules. Jack's chalet in Holiday Haven served as something of a second home, though he didn't get to stay there as often as he had before being crowned king. Back when he'd been more of a full-time resident, he used to race through the residential streets like some kind of crazed ice demon, but since becoming king, he'd agreed to keep his high-speed antics outside the town limits whenever he visited.

"See ya later, Corby! Lumi, a pleasure, as always. When you're bored with old stick-in-the-mud, give me a call!" With that, he tore off across the tundra, casting another spell to create a half-pipe up ahead. He zoomed up one side, then the other, before spinning the snowmobile in a full 360 turn—using another burst of his ice magic to stay suspended the extra moment.

"Idiot is going to get himself killed one of these days," Corbin muttered to himself as he stalked back to Ullr.

"I don't think there's anything you can do to stop him," I said softly. "He's not exactly big on the whole *listening* concept, is he?"

Corbin scoffed. "That's putting it mildly."

He shook his head. "Let's just hope he manages to have an heir before he breaks his neck, save me the trouble of having to take over the throne."

Little fingers of anxiety squeezed my heart at the thought. If Corbin ever became king, where would that leave me? The idea of being a princess was nerve-racking enough. To be queen would be downright terrifying.

I decided to buy Jack a proper helmet as soon as I could get to the store. And maybe I'd see if they could add a jumbo roll of packing bubbles to my order for good measure.

4

*B*y the time we returned to the barn, all that remained of the icy dome was a pile of shattered pieces. Astrid and the other renegade pixies were nowhere in sight. Sugarplum came hopping around the corner, his ears on high alert. "Lumi! You're back."

"What happened?" I asked.

Corbin bent and picked up one of the tiny candy canes the pixies had left behind. "I didn't even know they made them this small," he mused to himself.

Sugarplum's nose twitched as he stood up on his hind legs. "Some of the other pixies came not too long after you left. I tried to stop them, Lumi, but they banded together and dropped that shovel on top of the ice dome and it broke."

Glancing over my shoulder, I saw the broad shovel lying off to the side of where the dome had been. It was one I often used to muck out the reindeer stalls. "Great. Any idea where they went?"

Sugarplum looked down at his front feet, bent in front

of his furry chest. "They threw snowballs at me and then jetted off, back toward the woods. I wasn't fast enough to catch up to them."

"That's okay. Thanks for trying." I bent and scratched him between the ears until one of his back legs began thumping uncontrollably against the barn floor.

"Seems like the woods is the best place for them," Corbin said, pushing back to his full height. He tossed the tiny peppermint to the ground. "What's our next move? How do we get one of them to Doc Patches?"

I glanced at the wall to my right, where my staff leaned up against a stable door. "I could summon them with magic, but then we'd have a lot more than just one to deal with. We also need to figure out how we're going to travel back to the Pole. We need some kind of kennel ... or box."

"Does Sugarplum have a cage?" Corbin asked.

Sugarplum shot him a panicked look. "A cage! Why would I need a cage?"

I smiled. "No, definitely not. Sugarplum isn't a normal hare."

"Thank you, Lumi."

"I don't think we have anything around here, but we could make something." I left the barn and went a few yards out into the snow. My magic tended to work better outdoors, where I could be grounded in the snow and frost. With a few tries, I managed to conjure a pixie-sized cage from ice. One side was open, with the intention to seal it up once a pixie was inside. The question was how we were going to lure one away from the pack.

"You know, there's always one thing the pixies can't

resist," Sugarplum said, hopping around the cage to inspect it.

"Cocoa." A smile tugged at one corner of my mouth. "One pixie café coming right up."

With a flurry of magic, I formed a pixie-sized picnic table inside the box of ice. "I'll go get some cocoa. Sugarplum, do you think you could track down a pixie or two and let it slip there's free cocoa up here by the barn?"

My familiar didn't look thrilled by the assignment, but he nodded his head anyway. "I'll do my best. I just hope they don't get snow in my ears this time," he muttered.

Corbin and I watched Sugarplum hop around the side of the barn. "Tell you what, you stay here and I'll go get the cocoa. If you come inside, my mom will pounce on you to continue planning Jack's royal presser."

Corbin grinned. "Right. I probably should call the castle and let them know I've secured a venue."

"All right. I'll be right back."

I rushed inside and made a cup of cocoa using my family's long-held secret recipe—which may as well be frost pixie kryptonite—and raced back to the barn. Corbin was still on the phone with the castle, so I busied myself with the rest of the preparations. I placed the cocoa, piled high with whipped cream, on the table inside the makeshift cage, then retreated to the barn.

"Thank you, Freya," Corbin said before ending the call and slipping his phone back into his pocket. "Looks like Jack was telling the truth about what happened during his visit to Moonstone Isle," he told me. "Freya is my eyes and ears when I can't be there to supervise my brother."

I smiled. "Poor woman."

Corbin chuckled softly. "She's paid quite well, but even still, it's likely not enough."

"Probably not. Although I imagine babysitting a king will make for quite the line item on her future résumé," I teased.

Corbin ran a hand over his jaw, a smile still quirked on his lips. "Sometimes I wonder how this became my life. When Jack and I were young it all seemed too far away. We always knew the reality, of course, that one day he would take over as king, but now that it's here, I'm still not sure either of us fully knows what we're doing."

I took Corbin's hand. "It's a lot of responsibility, to be sure. But for what it's worth, I think you're doing a great job."

"Thanks, Lumi." He brushed the fingers of his free hand down the side of my face, his eyes locked on mine. "It's nice having days like this, where I can feel normal."

I laughed softly. "I'm not sure any of this is normal. I mean, we just baited an ice cage with hot cocoa to trap a feral frost pixie."

Corbin grinned and glanced over his shoulder at the cage. "You've got a point." He returned his gaze to me. "Still, there's nowhere else I'd rather be."

"You're sweet." Heat flushed my cheeks. "I'm happy I have someone on the days when things go a little bit sideways."

Corbin leaned in for a kiss, but before his lips met mine, the sound of someone clearing their throat interrupted. Breaking apart, we turned and found Sugarplum thumping one back leg impatiently. "You've got about three seconds before Astrid sucks down that entire mug of cocoa and flies away," he said.

I blinked, then raced to the doorway of the barn. Sure enough, inside the cage, Astrid hovered over the mug of cocoa, all but bathing herself in the mountain of whipped cream as she giggled over her good fortune of finding the sweet treat before the others did.

"That was fast," I whispered.

"Yeah, well, I found her dropping snowballs down your parents' chimney," Sugarplum said, giving the pixie a dirty look.

Cringing, I waved a hand and turned the nearby snow into a sheet of ice that neatly fit over the remaining opening. It took Astrid a moment to realize what had happened, but once she did, she let out a tiny scream and wrapped her hands around the frozen bars.

I stepped out of the barn and she locked her furious crystalline eyes with mine. "You did this?"

The betrayal in her voice cut through me. I got close and squatted down beside the cage. "It's for your own good, Astrid. I think something has happened to you and the others."

Astrid snarled and tore frantically at the bars, but it was futile. She wasn't strong enough to break through the ice and we would be gone before any of the other pixies could come to her aid.

"I'm sorry," I whispered. "I promise you'll be okay."

Astrid screamed and thrashed some more, managing to knock over the contents of the hot cocoa mug. I shored up the bottom with another layer of ice and managed to freeze the soupy chocolate before it could melt all the way through.

Straightening, I tried to shove the guilt aside. I'd known Astrid for most of my life, and I hated the idea of her being so angry with me. At the same time, the snarling, flailing pixie in the cage was nothing like the joyful, helpful pixie I knew. Her reaction only proved the point that something was seriously wrong.

"We can both ride on Ullr. I'll hold the cage on my lap," I said, turning back to Corbin.

He frowned. "Are you sure you'll be able to hold on? I can always call for a royal coach."

"I don't really want to draw any more attention than we already do."

"Ah. Understood." Corbin glanced at his winged steed, as if wishing there were some kind of seat belts attached to the saddle. "All right, then. Let's get going. But if at any point you feel unsteady, you have to tell me."

I smiled. "I promise I won't fall."

Corbin held the ice cage as I climbed onto Ullr's back, then he gently handed me the cage before climbing on in front of me. "Now we just have to hope this thing doesn't melt before we get to the North Pole."

"I'll think cold thoughts," I teased.

Corbin laughed and urged Ullr into flight.

* * *

WE ENDED up waiting for a little while in the clinic's lobby, but Mrs. Patches did her best to keep us occupied, telling us stories about some of their more memorable patients, which had apparently included a baby ice dragon that managed to give Doc Patches a mild case of frostbite as he'd treated the poor thing for a head cold.

When Doc Patches returned, he took both of us into the exam room, leaving his wife to close up the front. I placed the cage on the table and then stepped back to give the elf space to work. "Was everything all right with the reindeer?" I asked, while Doc Patches put on a pair of thick gloves—likely a safety precaution born in the aftermath of the baby ice dragon's accidental attack.

"Oh, yes. You know Santa. He dotes on them as if they were his own children," Doc Patches answered with a jolly chuckle. "Now, let's see," he leaned down and peeked in through the icy bars, "who do we have here?"

"This is Astrid," I answered.

The pixie shrieked and tried to reach out and take a swipe at Doc Patches' face. She managed to knock his glasses sideways before he pulled back. "My, my," he tutted. "Someone is quite unhappy."

Corbin and I exchanged a glance.

"And you said all of this started today?" Patches asked. "It came on suddenly, I mean?"

"Yes." I nodded. "They were on the farm yesterday, as late as eight, maybe nine. We were stringing up some new Christmas lights. The pixies always like to help, and they're quite useful for reaching the highest places."

"This was PM?" Doc Patches asked, glancing at me from over the top of his spectacles as he bent forward once more toward Astrid.

"Yes. PM. I didn't see them this morning while I was doing chores, but that's not unusual. They tend to sleep in, even more so in the off season. But Sugarplum said he saw a few of them fighting out in the field earlier today. It's not like them to fight over anything."

"Hmm." Doc Patches continued his visual inspection for a few moments in silence. When he straightened, he clasped his gloved hands together. "I think we might need a light sedative in order for me to run some tests. I don't expect she'd be willing to give me a blood sample as it is."

Proving his point, the pixie flashed her teeth and hissed.

"Astrid!" I shook my head. "I'm just at a loss. What could make a pixie act like this? It's like she's gone ... feral."

"My best guess is they all got into something, a plant or food perhaps, and whatever it is, it isn't mixing well with their magic. They feel out of sorts and that makes them grumpy. I can run a basic blood test and see if I can narrow down what we're dealing with."

I nodded. "Okay."

"We'll get to the bottom of this, Lumi," Doc Patches told me, giving my arm a reassuring pat. He moved to a tall cabinet beside the sink and opened the doors. Inside, a variety of tools were carefully arranged and labeled. He grabbed a net and then turned to position it along one side of the cage. "All right. Go ahead and let her loose."

Wincing, I strained to gather enough magic to melt a thin line around the perimeter of the wall of ice. When it broke free, Doc Patches let it fall to the ground and shatter. Astrid flew out of the cage, and while she was quick, she couldn't escape Doc Patches' net. He caught her with a quick swoop, then reached in and gently grasped her in one gloved hand. She struggled and fought, but her energy was nearly spent.

Doc Patches whispered an incantation in a language I didn't understand, and the pixie slowly relaxed and folded forward until she was sleeping, draped over Doc Patches' fingers. "There, there," he whispered with a kindly smile. "Rest easy, Astrid."

"That's a new one," I said.

The doctor smiled at me. "It's a simple relaxation spell. She was already quite exhausted. You have to have contact with the creature in order for it to work, otherwise I would have spared her the frustration of getting tangled in the net."

Corbin removed the ice cage from the exam table, then cast a quick wind to blow away the small puddle it left behind. Doc Patches smiled at him. "Quite handy, my dear boy. Thank you." He laid Astrid down on the table and began a more thorough investigation. He checked her pulse and then began looking over her tiny body for any sign of infection or injury.

Astrid carried a small satchel fashioned from leaves and pitch. It was just big enough that a single golf ball would fill it to capacity. Doc Patches removed the satchel and set it to one side. When he turned to gather the supplies needed for the blood draw, I reached over and picked up the bag. With careful fingers, I lifted the flap and dumped the contents out onto the table beside the sleeping pixie.

"It's just more of those tiny candy canes," I said, considering the half a dozen of them piled on the table. "I have no idea where these came from."

Corbin picked one up and pinched it between his thumb and forefinger. "Some kind of custom order, I'd imagine."

I started to say something, but my words trailed off as I realized there was something else in the satchel. A piece of thick paper was wadded up inside, and one corner was caught in between two leaves. "Wait a second," I said, prying it loose. It was a business card, folded into fourths to fit inside the tiny bag. I smoothed it out and gasped. "Corbin! Look at this."

There on the card, printed in glossy black ink:

Percy Lowell

Santa's Favorite Real Estate Agent

"Give me a jingle, and I'll make your house search jolly!"

5

"*That* rat!"

Doc Patches twisted around, his wispy brows raised. "Lumi, dear? Is everything all right?"

"I'm sorry, Doc, it's just … I think I might know what happened to the pixies." I glanced down at the card again. "Maybe he thought that if the pixies went berserk it would scare us off the property."

Patches looked to Corbin, his expression still befuddled.

"There's a real estate agent, Percy Lowell, who's been after a piece of the Northrop property," he explained to the vet before gesturing toward my hands. "This is his card. It was in Astrid's bag."

"And what about these candies?" Patches asked, considering the scattered treats. "Are they from him, too?"

"I'm not sure." I plucked one of them from the table. "Can you do any kind of test on it? See if it's been laced with something?"

Patches held out his hand, palm side up, and I dropped

the candy cane into his glove. "I'll certainly do my best." He cleared his throat. "Listen, it will take some time for me to examine the blood sample. Why don't you two head back to Holiday Haven? I'll call you in the morning. By then, I should have more information about what happened to our friend, here." He nudged his pointed chin at Astrid.

Corbin took my hand. "That sounds like a good idea. Thanks, Doc."

I hesitated, my gaze on the sleeping pixie. Corbin wrapped an arm around my waist, gently moving me toward the door, and I nodded. "Right. Of course."

I let Corbin lead the way out of the clinic, only stopping for a quick moment to say goodnight to Mrs. Patches. Outside, dusk was falling and the chill in the air had kicked up since the flight over. Corbin and I were both bundled up, but it was still a good idea to get out of the weather. "Are you hungry?" Corbin asked as we walked back to where Ullr was tethered. "We've missed our dinner reservations, but I'm sure we could find something else."

I gave a noncommittal hum as I glanced at the business card still in my hand. "It says he has an office, here in the Pole," I said after a moment. "Is he living here full time now?" I scoffed.

Corbin raised one thick eyebrow. "You're not considering going over there, are you?"

"I don't know." I frowned as I looked up the street. Things in the North Pole were always busy, or maybe it just seemed that way in comparison to the slower pace in Holiday Haven. Snowmobiles, sled dogs, and horses whizzed past, while owls and fairies swooped and dashed overhead as they went about their own errands. The postal system was heavily reliant on owls, making them a common sight, especially at this time of day.

In a couple of weeks, following the solstice, things would become even busier in both the North Pole and its suburbs, like Holiday Haven. The second half of the year always seemed to fly by in a flurry of activity and preparations, all culminating in the big night: Santa's flight. Christmas and the Yule Ball would come and go, and the cycle would begin again. It was a comfortable routine, but for some reason, standing there in the middle of it all, a twinge of anxiety pulsed through me. Almost as though things were happening too fast and too slow all at the same time.

"Let's go back to Holiday Haven," Corbin said, pulling me from my thoughts. "We don't want to jump to conclusions and make an already bad situation worse." He moved toward the candy-cane striped post and untied Ullr's reins. "Doc Patches will have more information for us in the morning. Then we can decide what to do next."

Reluctantly, I tucked the business card into the front pocket of my coat. "Don't you have to get back to the castle?"

A flicker of irritation passed over his face as he glanced at his watch, Ullr's reins hanging loose in his other hand. "I think I might stay in Holiday Haven tonight."

"Because of Jack?"

Corbin climbed onto Ullr's back, then reached for my

hand to help me up into the saddle behind him. "Precisely."

A smile tugged at my lips as I situated myself on Ullr's back, then looped my arms around Corbin's waist. I'd had the frozen pixie cage on my lap for the flight here, and it was nice to now be able to slide forward and hold onto his strong torso. "He seemed like he was behaving himself," I said, as Corbin prompted Ullr into motion. The horse began trotting down the street to build up speed, then lifted up, his powerful wings cutting through the frosty air. "At least he's keeping his promise about not riding his snowmobile through town."

Corbin scoffed. "That's a rather low bar. But yes, I suppose you're right."

I frowned. "Is there something else?"

I felt him exhale. "My father wants to see Jack married before his passing. His time in this realm is dwindling, and he's growing more impatient to see Jack settled, seeing as his plan to have him wed before his coronation didn't pan out."

"Aha. And I'm guessing Jack is still just as disinterested as before," I replied.

"He's changed a little, since what happened last winter, but I still can't see him settling down anytime soon. He'd rather be out on his snowmobile than going on proper dates, or tending to royal business."

I wasn't sure how to reply. Corbin tended to take on too much as it was, always serving as some kind of go-between for his brother and his father, something that had only intensified since his father's terminal diagnosis.

"Have you considered hiring some kind of matchmaker?" I asked. "Surely there has to be someone who could help."

Corbin laughed. "I'm fairly certain Jack would send them running from the castle within thirty minutes. He wouldn't exactly be a cooperative client."

"Who says he has to know?" I asked.

"What do you mean?"

"Hire the matchmaker, give them all of the qualities Jack would want, and let them do the rest. Think of it like a professionally arranged blind date!"

Corbin considered it for a moment. "It's not a bad idea. The question is, what kind of woman could make Jack change his mind about living life as a permanent bachelor?"

"Hmm. I think with Jack it's about the chase, so maybe someone who isn't interested in him would be the key. Someone who he has a lot in common with, but who isn't initially interested in him, or even better, someone who doesn't even know who he is."

"So, essentially, I need to find him a snowmobile mechanic who loves beer, darts, and bad karaoke, who also happens to be from another country and/or is independently wealthy and not interested in chasing after a royal crown?" Corbin said, laughing as he got toward the end of the laundry list of qualifications.

I giggled. "Yeah, exactly. I mean, how hard can that really be?"

We laughed as we soared out of the North Pole, the sound echoing across the wild tundra.

* * *

ULLR TOUCHED down near the open-air rink in the center of town. The outdoor market was shuttered for the season but there were still a lot of people milling about the town square, enjoying the crisp evening. A few vendors had year-round carts where they sold treats, and the smell of kettle corn and roasted chestnuts called out to me like a siren's song, reminding me that I hadn't had anything other than half a glass of lemonade since that morning before I'd started my chores. I often forgot to eat while working on the farm, opting for a large breakfast and dinner, with only a handful of snacks throughout the day—though I usually ended up sharing those with the reindeer, not always by choice.

Corbin waited for me to dismount before following, then he took Ullr's reins in one hand and my hand in his other one. "So, what sounds good? Looks like there are a few options out here, but I think something indoors would be better."

"Agreed." As I was considering the nearby restaurants, a flurry of activity caught my eye. The fairies I'd seen on our way out of town were still performing for a dwindling crowd around the ice rink. "I wonder what that's all about," I commented.

Corbin didn't hear me, his mind locked in on finding a meal. Not that I could blame him. Based on the rumbling of my own stomach, I should focus on the mission, too. Still, it was odd to have such a lengthy impromptu performance. Normally, formal events were advertised around town but I hadn't seen anything about this one.

"How about Wet Your Wassail?" Corbin suggested with a grin. "We know that place is now a Jack-free zone."

I turned my head away from the fairies on the rink and nodded in agreement. "Sure."

Since being kidnapped and stowed away in the pub's basement, Jack hadn't returned to what was once his favorite haunt in Holiday Haven. I figured he'd eventually return as they served the best lager in town, but for now, we could guarantee he wouldn't pop up to interrupt our meal.

"When is the next open mic night?" I asked as we headed over to the pub. "Are you going to play?"

Corbin shrugged. "I don't know. Maybe."

Grinning, I nudged my arm into his. "You should. As much as Sugarplum and I have enjoyed our private concerts, it would be fun to see you perform for a real crowd."

Corbin smiled down at me. "I'll think about it."

The English-style pub was a quick walk from the center of town, and within a few minutes we were shrugging out of our heavy coats and being shown to a corner booth. The darkened interior made it an ideal place for us to enjoy a meal, away from prying eyes. Most people at the pub were seated around the bar, while the establishment's owner, a vampire named Clarence Griswold, held court, slinging drinks and telling jokes.

Corbin handed me a menu and we settled into a familiar discussion of what to order. Moments like this made it easy to forget who I was with. At the pub, on a chilly weeknight, chatting about the various merits of mozzarella sticks versus onion rings, we were just any other young couple. Nothing special or out of the ordinary.

We enjoyed a pair of drinks with our appetizer, and before our entrees were brought out, Corbin slipped away to the restroom. I noticed our drinks were low and wandered over to the bar to say hello to Clarence and order a round of refills. "Well, good evenin', Lumi," the vampire said with a flourish of an Oxford English accent.

"Hello, Clarence," I replied with a smile. "Another round, when you get a chance."

Clarence slapped one hand on the bar. "Coming right up!"

Rudy Portsmith, one of the pub's regulars, turned toward me, one hand resting on his glass. "How are things at the ranch?" he asked.

I smiled politely and resisted the urge to correct him. "Oh, you know, always gearing up for the busy season."

"I heard that scoundrel Percy's been after your parents," he replied with a grin. "I hope you sent him packing with a blast of ice right to the keester!"

"Believe me, I wish I could." I laughed. "Where did you hear about that, anyway?"

Rudy glanced at the man on his other side. "When was that, Merv? Two, three nights ago?"

Merv, an elderly gentleman with a balding head of gray hair, twisted his face as he considered the question. "Hmm, must have been Tuesday. He was in here, bragging about being on the cusp of his biggest deal yet. Of course, once he said it was about your farm, none of us believed him. We know your family will never sell."

Clarence returned with my drinks. "You're right to be careful, Lumi," he told me, placing them on the bar in front of me. "Percy is not to be trifled with. Gus O'Neal, one of my regulars, is stuck in a battle with him and the town council over a property dispute. Percy's trying to buy up a strip of homes over on Douglas Fir Drive, wants to gut them and convert the whole street into a commercial zone. Gus was the last holdout. Next thing he knows, there's a series of mysterious complaints being registered against him with the town council, claiming he was in violation of various codes. Gus did a little investigatin' and found it was Percy, trying to get him tossed out."

"That's awful!" I exclaimed, taking the two drinks.

Rudy patted my shoulder. "You hang tough. Don't let him win this one. We're all behind you."

Beside him, Merv nodded in agreement.

"Thanks. I appreciate that."

With a nod, I turned and took the drinks back to the corner booth, where Corbin was already waiting. "Thank you," he said as I slid into the seat beside him. I quickly caught him up on what I'd heard at the bar. "Seems like he isn't opposed to playing dirty," Corbin said when I finished.

"The question is, how dirty," I added. "If my hunch is right, and he tried to hurt the pixies, I'll take this all the way to Santa himself if I have to."

Corbin squeezed my hand. "We both will."

6

*D*oc Patches called bright and early the next morning. I was about three sips into my morning coffee, listening to Sugarplum as he hopped around the kitchen, rattling off a laundry list of antics the pixies got into after I left with Corbin. According to him, they'd swarmed back into the barn and proceeded to rain down mayhem until Mom chased them out with a push broom.

I had no doubt Mom would repeat Sugarplum's account—likely with a lot more fury—as soon as I poked my head out of my cabin, so I wasn't in a huge hurry to get ready and leave for my daily chores. Doc Patches' call was a welcome interruption to my usual morning routine.

"Thanks for calling," I told him.

"Well, Lumi, it looks like whatever is making the pixies go wild is indeed linked to those candy canes you found," Doc Patches told me. "I melted one down to run some tests, and the heat seems to have released some foreign ingredient. Instead of melting into a pink or red puddle, it changed to a dark green."

"Dark green?" I frowned. "What would make it do that?"

The sound of dishes clanging together rattled in the background. "I'm not sure," Doc Patches replied, seemingly unaware of the noise he was making. "This isn't my area of expertise, I'm afraid. I've put in a few calls to some healer friends, they might have a better idea. But for now, I'd say there is something in those candies, and if I were you, I'd get them away from the rest of the pixies as quickly as possible. Depending on what type of contaminant we're dealing with, it might work itself out of their systems once the substance is no longer being ingested, although judging by our friend, Astrid, I'm not too sure that will be the case."

I winced. "She's still acting up?"

"Afraid so," the doc replied, his tone sorrowful. "She awoke from the magic-induced sleep angrier than before. I've put her back under for the time being. I'll try waking her once more in another six hours and see if I can't get her to eat something else. Until I know what kind of spell or poison we're dealing with, I won't be able to provide a full course of treatment."

"I understand. Thank you, Doc. I'll do my best to get the candies away from the others." I glanced down at my hand and wondered how many fingers I might lose in the process.

"Very good. I will phone back later with any updates," Doc Patches said. "Take care of yourself, Lumi."

"You, too, Doc."

We ended the call and I recapped the information to the eager Sugarplum. His ears flopped when I explained we still didn't have an answer. "How are we supposed to get those candy canes away from them?" he asked.

"I'm not sure." I drank deeply from my coffee mug, turning over a few strategies, though none of them sounded like they'd be very fun.

When I set aside the coffee, I reached for my phone again.

"Who are you going to call now?" Sugarplum asked.

"The person who might have the answers to this whole thing," I said, my jaw squared as I went to the coat rack by the front door of my small cabin. I fished the business card from the front pocket of the coat I'd worn the night before.

Sugarplum followed closely on my heels. "Who's that?" he asked.

"Percy Lowell," I replied, already tapping the number into my phone before my nerves talked me out of it.

An answering machine picked up the call, rattling off Percy's slogan and instructions to leave a message, which I did, keeping the details sparse. I hung up the call and placed my phone back on the table.

Sighing, I slid a glance down at Sugarplum. "Guess I can't avoid the inevitable any longer."

The hare hopped to the door and stood to his full height, balanced on his large hind feet. "Let's go kick some pixie tushie!"

I smiled and downed the last dregs of coffee from my mug. "We're not going to fight with them, Sugarplum."

"You say that now …," the hare muttered.

After bundling up and pulling on my winter boots, I grabbed my staff and headed out into the elements. It was my favorite kind of morning, with a clear sky and rays of sunlight gently bouncing off the untouched snow that had fallen overnight. Unfortunately, I'd barely drawn in a full breath of the crisp air before a shriek echoed from the barn. Sugarplum scampered toward the scream and I darted after him. We were halfway there when my mom came barreling out, her arms over her head to ward off the swarm of pixies flying after her, angrily tossing handfuls of black pellets.

"Sweet Mother Nature," I groaned, raising my staff. I threw a shield of ice in an effort to block the worst of it.

"You have to stop them, Lumi!" Mom exclaimed as she raced around the side of the barn. "They broke into the kitchen while I was bringing in the groceries, and they ran off with all of the bags!"

"Even the carrots?" Sugarplum cried.

In reply, a pixie swooped over the hare, cackling wildly as they made a point to nibble on a baby carrot.

Sugarplum leaped at the pixie, but wasn't quick enough. The pixie blew a raspberry and surged back into the air. Other pixies darted around, showing off their haul: a variety of other household staples. Most of the items were heavy enough they required multiple pixies to carry them away, and I lost count of how many were zipping to and from the barn.

Cringing, I peeked inside. Groceries lay scattered across the floor. Some pixies weren't bothering to take the food back to the safety of the woods, instead opting to crack open cans of soda and bags of chips right there on the barn floor. A few pixie feet stuck out of a bag of cheesy puffs. Across the way, two hovered over an open can of soda and were taking turns filling their hands with the fizzy brown liquid.

They were everywhere, and if anything they seemed more feral than the day before, no longer using words to communicate with me or each other. They snarled and squawked at one another to make their fury known. Marble-sized snowballs and reindeer pellets whizzed through the air in equal proportions as they fought over the treasure trove. I shouted, trying to get them to leave, but it only seemed to anger them further.

The reindeer were still in their stalls, letting out nervous sounds and stamping their feet as the pixies flew over them. I exhaled and charged into the barn, managing to get the reindeer stalls open and evacuated before retreating back outside where it was safer. Mucking stalls would have to wait.

As for the groceries … that was a lost cause.

I heaved the heavy door closed, trapping the majority of the pixies inside the barn—at least, for a little while. "What a disaster," I exclaimed, bracing my back against the door as pixies hit the other side. "They're even worse today!"

"I didn't see any candy canes," Sugarplum said. "Did you?"

I considered it, then shook my head. "Maybe they ran out? Do you know where they even came from? We don't order ones that small."

During the peak of tourist season we went through crates of the things, but up until yesterday, I hadn't even realized they came in such tiny sizes. The pixies hadn't gotten them from the storage shed, that much was certain.

Mom came down from her refuge on the porch and met me at the gate to the pasture. "Looks like I'll need to go back to the market," she grumbled, peering past my shoulder toward the barn. "Pandora Ashmore called while they were ravaging the kitchen. She wanted to know how long the pixies' performance runs, since she's putting together the program for the solstice party."

I scrubbed hand down my face. "That's right. What did you tell her?"

"I told her the pixies were under the weather, and that I would call her back tomorrow to let her know if they will be able to perform."

"They've been looking forward to it for weeks now," I said, sighing heavily as I looked back at the barn.

"She said they have some other troupe who can stand in, if need be. The Poinsettia Performers, I believe was the name."

"Hmm. Never heard of them." I shrugged. "Listen, don't worry about the groceries. I can pick things up on my way back home later today."

"You're going into town?"

"Corbin wound up staying in Holiday Haven last night, so I'm going to see him before he has to head back to the castle."

Mom's eyes twinkled, as she momentarily forgot about the mess of pixies. "You two make a sweet couple. The entire town thinks so. Imagine, when you become a princess. My daughter! Full-blown royalty!"

"Okay, Mom," I said with a strained laugh. "Let's not

go there. We're taking things slow. No one is in a rush."

"Mhmm. I've seen the way he looks at you, Lumi. Like you're the only witch in the entire world." Mom smiled.

My cheeks warmed and I cleared my throat. "I should get busy. The reindeer need to be fed before I leave."

"Oh, your father can do that," Mom said, flapping a hand. "You go see Corbin. Tell him to give me a call when he wants to talk about Jack's event. I already told all of my friends. They're green with envy! Oh, that reminds me, I'll need to call Viv and have her start working on some dresses for us."

"Mom," I groaned, but it was too late. She was already scurrying back toward the house, muttering happily to herself, "Oooh, I can just see it now. Sweetheart neckline, cap sleeves. Gold? Or silver? Maybe both!"

* * *

I CALLED Corbin and we made plans to meet in the town square. I said goodbye to Sugarplum, ran a comb through my hair, and saddled up Starlea, who was all too happy to leave the barn behind and go for a flight. We touched down outside the Candy Cane Café and I popped inside to order two cocoas to go. Then, with Starlea keeping pace beside me, we walked to the town square to wait for Corbin. The ice rink had a few early morning skaters, most of whom seemed like professionals, judging by the way they whizzed and leaped along with the cheery music piped out from the speakers stationed around the rink. I found an empty bench nearby and settled in to watch them practice as I enjoyed my cocoa.

After a while, I started to wonder what was keeping Corbin. Setting his cocoa to the side, I dug my phone out of my pocket. There weren't any messages or missed calls from him, but after another minute, it buzzed in my gloved hand. It wasn't Corbin's name on the screen, though. Instead, it was an unknown number with a North Pole area code.

"Hello?" I answered.

"Is this Lumi Northrop?" a male voice asked.

"It is. Who is this?"

"Percy Lowell, returning your call."

"Oh." My stomach squirmed. I'd been full of bravado when I'd made the call to his office earlier that morning, but now my courage had deflated back to its normal size. "Right. I need to speak with you about my parents' property."

"Glad to hear it!"

I glanced at my phone to see the time. "I'm in Holiday Haven now, it will take me a little while to get to your office—"

"You're in luck!" Percy interjected. "It just so happens that I've recently expanded into a satellite office, here in Holiday Haven. Business has been booming, and you know how tiresome it is commuting back and forth from the Pole all the time. I'm just down on Gingerbread Lane. You can't miss me."

"Oh. Okay." My hand clenched the phone a little tighter. "Well, then I guess I'll be there shortly."

"Looking forward to it."

The call ended and I stuffed my phone back into my pocket. Glancing around the square, I still saw no sign of

Corbin. He was almost fifteen minutes late, which wasn't like him. A band of fairies flew onto the skating rink, chatting excitedly as they hovered in a circle and sipped from small cups of cocoa. They were larger than the pixies, probably closer to Sugarplum in size, but their movements and mannerisms were similar.

I watched them for another few minutes in between scanning the square for Corbin. At one point, a dark-haired fairy flew over to join the circle; she said a few words and the other fairies cheered before she quickly buzzed off in the opposite direction.

I didn't want to go to Percy's office alone, but at the same time, I was impatient to get answers. Astrid and the other pixies were counting on me. "Looks like you'll need to be my backup, Starlea," I told the reindeer as I got to my feet. I picked up Corbin's cocoa and headed toward Gingerbread Lane.

I was rounding the corner when I heard my name. "Lumi!"

I turned and saw Corbin jogging across the square.

"I'm so sorry," he said, coming to a stop when he reached me. "I went to see Jack, and he was ... well, being Jack."

"It's okay. Here," I pressed the cocoa into his gloved hand. "Got this for you. It might be a little lukewarm though."

"Thank you." Corbin looked up at the street sign. "Where were you headed?"

"We're going to pay a visit to the North Pole's hardest hustling real estate agent."

7

*P*ercy Lowell's office was almost exactly as I would have pictured it, had I ever bothered to try. It sat wedged between a hair salon and a daycare center. The salon and daycare were decked out, their windows bursting with color and Christmas-time wonder. In stark contrast, Percy's shopfront looked like something designed by an ad executive for a luxury perfume brand. Expensive blown-glass black and white ornaments hung along the top of the windows flanking the front door. The only other sign that it was in any way festive were the miniature wreaths on the front doors of the model condominium building placed in the right display window.

"I see he's really immersing himself in the holiday spirit," I muttered. "And what is this? 'Merry Meadows'?" I jabbed a finger at the glass. "Where's he going to put this monstrosity? Is he planning on bulldozing the art museum for this? Or maybe he'll just pave over the ice rink, I mean, really, that's frivolous, isn't it?"

Corbin opened the door. "Let's go and ask him."

With a resolute nod, I bustled into the office.

The interior was even colder than the front windows. Marble floors, metal-framed furnishings, everything in muted neutral tones. No sign of a Christmas tree or even a sprig of holly.

A fairy sitting at the desk poked her head up at our arrival. She smiled briefly, but there was no warmth to it. "May I help you?"

"We're here to see—"

"I see you found the place all right," Percy interjected, stepping into the short hallway that formed a cul-de-sac of three doors. He saw Corbin over my shoulder and his salesman grin faltered for a moment before he fixed it back in place. "Come, come. Can I get you anything? Coffee, tea, water, juice? I have a cold-pressed guava-mint that's to die for!"

"We're fine," Corbin replied.

Percy steepled his fingers together before stepping through the doorway to the right. "Straight to business, then."

"He has guava-mint juice, but no cocoa? Does this guy even know where he is?" I hissed over my shoulder at Corbin as we crossed the reception space.

He smiled and placed a hand on my back. "I know, absolutely beastly."

We stepped into Percy's office—which seemed to serve as some kind of personal shrine to his achievements. The bookcases lining the far wall held not a single book, but instead their shelves served as a display case for a dozen plaques and crystal trophies, intermixed with framed

63

photographs of Percy in a variety of flashy suits, posing with people equally as dressed up.

"As you can see, I've enjoyed quite a career thus far," Percy said as I wandered closer to the shelves.

Frowning, I turned away. "So, why come here? Why Holiday Haven? Why the North Pole? You have the entire world, and yet you come here."

"I sense you don't approve," Percy said, adjusting his necktie as he took his seat in a plush leather chair behind a large desk.

"Do you even like Christmas?" I asked.

Percy shrugged one shoulder. "Sure. Doesn't everyone?"

I stared at him, unsure how to respond.

"We didn't come here to discuss your various real estate ventures," Corbin interjected.

"No?" Percy looked wounded.

"No," Corbin replied firmly. "We want to know if you've spoken to any of the frost pixies that live on the Northrop property."

"Pixies?" Percy repeated, his voice an octave higher, as though this were the first he was hearing of such a creature.

"The frost pixies live in the frozen woods on the back acreage of my parents' land," I said, finding my voice once more. "One of them was carrying your business card, and I can assure you, we pitch them into the fire as soon as you leave, so she didn't get it from us."

Percy's eyes narrowed slightly. "I *may* have struck up a conversation with a pixie or two on one of my visits to check out the property. What difference does it make? I know they aren't on the deed. They can't sell the property out from under your family."

"What about gifts?" I asked. "Candy canes, specifically. Tiny ones."

Percy leaned back in his chair, one hand clenched around an expensive-looking pen. "I don't know. I send gifts to a lot of people. Clients, potential clients, et cetera."

"Fair enough," Corbin replied, "but we're specifically interested in the pixies."

Percy considered us for a moment. "I *believe* a basket of candy canes, custom ordered to size, was sent out about a week ago."

"For what reason? You just acknowledged they have no power to sell the property to you."

Percy exhaled as he sat forward, dropping the pen in favor of lacing his fingers together in front of him on the desk. "I thought perhaps they might prove to be an ally in persuading your parents to sell. I promised their lands would remain untouched if they agreed to help me secure the sale. I don't think it did any good. The one I talked to had the attention span of my ex-wife at a pop-up shoe sale." Percy's jaw flexed. "Anyway, they mentioned they liked candy, so I had my confectioner send a batch to them."

My mouth dropped open. "You have your own confectioner?"

"Well, no, but I'd say I make up a good fifty percent of Hailey's profits, at present."

"And there was no funny business? With the candy, I mean."

Percy frowned. "I'm not sure I follow. Funny business?"

I glanced at Corbin, wondering if it was wise to spill the details of the entire ordeal. "The candy canes were contaminated," Corbin said, shifting his gaze to the slick agent. "You don't know anything about that?"

"Contaminated? Of course not! Why would I intentionally give anyone rotten candy? I'm trying to make a deal here."

As much as I hated to admit it, his reaction sounded sincere. He'd either missed his calling as an actor, or he was telling us the truth.

"Did something happen to the pixies?" Percy asked. "Are they all right?"

"They will be," I said, hoping I was right. "But you need to stay away from them. And from my parents. I know you think you can eventually name some price or try some trick and get your way, but I'm here to tell you that's not the case. The sanctuary has been passed down for generations of Northrops, and you aren't going to end that tradition."

"All I am asking for is a small parcel," Percy insisted. "Currently unused land, just sitting there."

"To you it might look unused, but the frozen wood is its own kind of sanctuary. Wild reindeer, hares, birds, pixies, sprites." I shook my head. "You cannot have any of it. Give it up now, or I will have no choice but to take my concerns to Santa Claus."

"Santa Claus?" Percy's lips thinned. "And what makes you think he would get involved in a real estate spat?"

Smiling, I lifted my chin. "We care for his retired reindeer, each one just as special to him as if they were of his own blood. Additionally, we raise the reindeer that will eventually join his elite team. If I put a little bug in his ear that someone is bothering my family and attempting to interfere with our important work ... well, you tell me if you think he would get involved."

Percy's face flushed, the knuckles of his interlaced hands going white.

Corbin smiled at me as he moved to the door, pausing to glance back at the seething real estate agent. "Oh, and before we go, we're going to need the name of that confectioner."

Percy waved a dismissive hand. "Pia will get it for you on the way *out*," he growled.

"Good day, Mr. Lowell," I said, barely holding back a grin.

I'd actually done it! I'd stood up for myself and didn't get tangled over my words or mumble. For once, I'd said all of the things I thought, instead of letting them get jumbled.

"You were great," Corbin whispered as we went back down the short hallway to the reception area.

Pia, the fairy at the front desk, barely glanced up. "Have a nice day," she said.

"Before we go, we need the name and number of the confectioner who sent the candy canes to the frost pixies," Corbin said.

Pia frowned. "I see ... you won't mind if I go and speak with Mr. Lowell for just a moment."

She didn't bother to wait for our reply, already flitting away from the desk.

Corbin leaned against the desk and grinned at me. "Your family should send you to law school and put you in charge of the sanctuary's legal matters."

I laughed. "I think that might be a little overzealous, but thank you."

He chuckled. "Well, if they won't, just know the castle could always use a talented spokesperson."

I smiled, but something about the statement pricked at me, though I wasn't quite sure why. There wasn't time to sort it out either. Pia flew back in like a gust of north wind sent her flying back out of Percy's office. She hurried to flip through the pages of a large book on the desk and jotted down some information on a small square of paper.

Her violet eyes were shadowed as she lifted them to hand me the paper. "Here you are."

"Thank you." I slid the note into my pocket.

We started to leave, when the fairy squeaked out a timid, "Wait!"

Pia glanced toward her boss's open door, then flew in a little closer. "You work at the reindeer sanctuary?" she asked me.

I nodded.

She wrung her tiny hands together. "Is it true the pixies won't be performing at the solstice celebration?"

"I—I don't know yet."

"But it's true that they're sick? Right?" she asked, the words rushed.

"Y-yes, but I don't know how long until they're back to normal."

Pia smiled in a way far more genuine than when she'd

greeted us. She managed to temper the edges of the grin as she brought her gaze back to mine. "*So* sorry to hear that. You'll have to send them our best."

"Our?" I repeated.

Pia nodded, her wings beating together to lift her a few inches from her seat. "Yes, the—"

Percy Lowell stormed out of his office, his overcoat draped across one arm. "Pia, I'm going to—" He stopped abruptly when he saw us still standing at the desk. His eyes flashed. "Was there something else?" he snapped.

"No. Thank you." I gave Pia one more glance, then turned and went out the shop's front door.

We stepped out onto Gingerbread Lane and found Starlea basking in the attention of a few local townspeople. A woman glanced up from stroking Starlea's neck and her eyes went wide. "I knew it! Barbie, see, it *is* her!"

Hot panic crawled up my throat and into my cheeks. I reached for Corbin's free hand. "Hello," he said to the onlookers. "If you'll excuse us—"

"Prince Corbin! Can you sign this for me?" a woman asked, presenting him with the back of a wrinkled receipt.

Corbin looked just as uncomfortable with the flurry of attention as I was and shook his head. "I'm sorry. Not today."

I dropped Corbin's hand long enough to gather Starlea's reins. She was well-behaved enough that I didn't need to lead her along in order to get her to follow us, but I feared someone else might grab them and try to keep us hostage until they snapped our picture or got an autograph.

I ducked my chin and we hurried away at a brisk clip.

When we reached the town square, I dared to glance over my shoulder and found that most of the townspeople had gone back to their errands.

"I'm sorry about all of that, Lumi," Corbin said when we were clear of them.

"It's not your fault," I told him.

"Well, that's not technically true. If you weren't with me, you'd be able to wander through town unbothered."

He was right, but I didn't want to rub it in. "It makes me feel bad for Jack," I said, hoping to lighten the mood, "and that's not something I ever thought I would say."

Corbin smiled, but it didn't quite reach his eyes. "Yeah, I suppose he's had to deal with this level of attention and scrutiny for a lot longer than either of us."

"Maybe that's why he acts out," I said, more as an afterthought. "Maybe he figures since he's going to get their attention anyway, he might as well give them something to talk about."

Corbin chuckled. "Come on, now. Let's not go painting him as that much of a sympathetic character. He's a scoundrel. He acts up because he wants to."

I nodded, but there was a part of me that held onto the question for further consideration.

"Speaking of, though, I don't have much time before I need to get back to the castle," Corbin continued. "What are you going to do? Will you go speak with the confectioner?"

I exhaled. "I don't know. I guess I could, but I'm not sure what she'll be able to tell me. It's not like some random candy maker would poison a batch of candy canes. So, unless I find some other link between her and the pixies, it seems like it might be a waste of time."

"What did you make of the fairy at the desk? Pia. Was it just me, or did she seem a little *too* happy at the idea of the pixies being unavailable to perform at the solstice?"

"What I don't know is how she even heard about anything regarding the pixies," I said, before the answer smacked me in the face a half-second later. "Mrs. Patches," I said with a slight groan. "She means well, of course, but figgy pudding, isn't there such a thing as doctor-patient confidentiality?"

"I think that might be just for people," Corbin replied with a sympathetic look.

"I suppose it could have also been that party-planner. Pandora? My mom spoke with her on the phone earlier, but she just told her the pixies weren't up for a rehearsal. I don't think she told her the extent of it."

We walked across the cobblestone square, each lost in thought. Out on the ice rink, the band of fairies I'd seen earlier had finished their coffee break and were performing once more for a crowd of onlookers. Their pixie dust floated through the air, making delicate patterns before falling to freeze under their skates.

"Wait ...," I said, stopping in my tracks. "I saw her—she was here—she was with them." I pointed at the rink. "I thought she looked familiar, but I couldn't place her until just now."

Corbin gave me a confused look. "What do you mean? Who?"

"Pia. When I was waiting for you to get here, I saw her go up to those fairies before they started performing. She said something and they all got really excited, then she flew off. Right in the direction of Gingerbread Lane." It all fit together.

Dropping Corbin's hand and Starlea's reins, I hurried across the square and approached the ice rink. "Excuse me!" I called out to the nearest fairy as she lifted off the ground to do a flip in the air. She bobbled and nearly crashed into the fairy beside her.

"Larella, be careful!" that fairy said, fluttering her wings as she zoomed away.

The fairy I'd beckoned flitted toward me, her fair cheeks tinged with a rosy shade of pink. "Yes?" she said.

I twinkled my fingers at her. "Hi, sorry to interrupt, but what is the name of your troupe? I've been watching all morning and would love to see a full performance someday."

"Oh!" The fairy beamed. "We're the Poinsettia Performers. You'll be able to see us do the full routine at the summer solstice celebration! We just got word this morning we were selected to participate! Isn't that so exciting? I can hardly believe it myself, to tell you the truth."

"Glorietta, what are you doing?" another fairy snapped from across the ice. "You're not in formation!"

"Oops. I'd better go," she said. "See you at the solstice party!"

8

"*I*t was them! It makes perfect sense," I exclaimed after racing back to Corbin to explain my new theory. "With the frost pixies out of the way, they get to perform at the celebration. If that's not motive—well, I don't know what is."

"Okay, okay. Slow down," Corbin said. "We've got one problem."

"What?"

"How did they screw with the candy canes?"

"Pia! She probably hand-delivered them for her slimy boss. She never thought the suspicion would twist back on her."

Corbin nodded. "I guess that makes sense. So, how do we prove it? She doesn't strike me as the confession type, and everything else is circumstantial at best."

"I think we can go and speak with Hailey, the candy maker, and confirm that Pia made the delivery. That might be enough to get the HHPD involved. If they can find the contaminant in Pia's house, they'll have to arrest her." I dug into my coat pocket and pulled out two of the small candy canes. "And when we go see the police, we can turn these over to them so they can start figuring out exactly what kind of poison we're dealing with."

Seething, I glared back at the Poinsettia Performers as they tumbled and dove through their routine.

"Hey, hey lovebirds!"

I twisted back around to find Jack sauntering across the square, two royal guards in tow. He flashed us a jovial smile. "Anyone else think we should have brunch before Corby and I have to leave? I'd kill for a mimosa right about now. Lumi, you look like a mimosa fan, name the place and we'll go. On me."

I wasn't sure how to take the statement. I shook my head and was about to protest, to tell him we were busy, when Jack reached out and swiped the candy canes from my hand. "Don't mind if I do!" he said, tossing them into his mouth. He crunched down and swallowed before Corbin or I could fully react. "Hmm. A little on the small side, but the mint flavor is nice and strong. I give it four stars," he said.

"Jack!" Corbin growled. "You absolute dolt!"

"What?" Jack said, still grinning.

Suddenly, his smile widened and something sparked in his blue eyes. With a flick of his hand, a perfectly formed snowball appeared in his palm. Laughing, he jogged backward a few paces. "Watch out, Corby!" he cried out, before slinging the ball right at his brother's face.

Corbin shot a blast of north wind at the snowball, breaking it apart before it reached him. "Knock it off, Jack."

74

"Hmm. Well, if you don't want to play, I'm sure someone else will. Lumi? Are you game?" His eyes gleamed as he conjured another snowball.

Corbin swore loudly and tugged my wrist to pull me behind him. He broke the second snowball just as easily as the first, but Jack managed to reload a lot quicker, and began firing them in quick bursts, two, then three at a time.

In retaliation, Corbin took Jack's legs out with a gust of wind. Jack responded by icing over the cobblestones under Corbin's feet, sending him crashing to the ground on his rear end. With a snarl, Corbin smacked Jack with another blast of wind, driving him backwards a few feet as he attempted to stand. Jack laughed before he drew both hands to send a fresh round of snowballs at his brother's head. Corbin used a whip of air to send them back at Jack.

The brothers' tussle quickly turned into a public spectacle, something akin to a Pay-Per-View fight night, as people poured into the square from the surrounding homes and shops to watch.

When Jack fashioned sharp icicles to throw at Corbin, I panicked and used my own magic to join the fray. Just as before, with the pixies, I conjured a wall of ice to stand between the brothers. Ten feet high and seven—then eight —feet wide. Jack was delighted by my participation. "Oh, this makes me want to get my snowmobile! Lumi, see if you can set up a ramp going over the town hall building. I'll bet I can jump it if you give me enough runway!"

"Enough!" I shouted, ignoring his plea. "This is the candy canes' fault!" I said, looking to Corbin.

Jack scoffed and turned to his guards. "Come on!" he said. "Change of plans!"

With a heavy sigh, Corbin sent one last blast of wind at his brother, this time spinning him around to face us. "Snap out of it, Jack."

"Out of what? I'm just having a little fun," Jack replied, already working on another snowball.

I held up a hand, ready to intercede again, but before Jack could fire, he stopped and blinked a few times in rapid succession, as though he'd just gotten an eyelash stuck in one eye.

"Jack?" I asked. "Are you all right?"

The Frost King let the snowball fall from his fingertips and it landed with a *splat* on the cobblestone plaza. "What in the—"

Corbin lowered his hand and walked slowly toward his brother. "It wore off that quickly?" he asked, glancing at me.

"I—I guess so. He only ate two of them, and he is a lot bigger than a pixie." I paused and frowned. "It's weird though, Percy said he sent the candy canes to the pixies a week ago. But if they work this quickly, why did it take so long for us to see the change in behavior? Believe me, there's no way they held off on eating them. Candy—of any variety—doesn't last long around the pixies."

"Maybe they didn't find them right away. After all, it's not like they have a proper mailing address. Maybe Pia just left the package in the woods, waiting for one of them to stumble upon the treats."

I nodded, piecing it together. "Yeah, maybe."

"What are you two prattling on about?" Jack asked,

rubbing the side of his head where he'd taken a particularly hard rebound shot from one of his own snowballs.

"The candy canes you just ate were laced with some kind of poison," Corbin explained. "Serves you right, stealing candy from someone without asking. Do you do this kind of thing all the time?" Corbin shook his head. "Do we need to get you one of those royal food tasters? Someone to follow you around and run spells on everything that goes in your mouth, to make sure it hasn't been tampered with?"

Jack grumbled darkly under his breath, "I think I have more than enough babysitters as it is, *dear* brother."

Corbin stared at Jack for another long moment, before breaking contact. He gestured for the guards. "Go on without me. I have some business to finish here in town. I'll be back to the castle by this evening."

"Yes, your grace," the guard on the left replied, ducking his head.

Jack plastered his smile back in place and waved to the townspeople as they began going back to whatever they'd been doing before the sibling brawl, but there was a cold chill behind his eyes as he fell into step behind the guards and left the plaza.

"Yikes," I said to Corbin once Jack was out of earshot. "Do you think maybe you should go clear the air with him?"

Corbin's jaw flexed as he watched his brother walk away. "I'll speak with him tonight. Privately. Right now there are too many people watching."

"If you need to go, I understand."

Slowly, he returned his attention to me. "We'll go and

speak with the candy maker. If we're correct, we can file everything with the police department and then I'll return home."

I nodded. "Okay. At least we know the poison should eventually work its way out of the pixies' systems, at least, based on what happened to Jack. I'll call Doc Patches and let him know what happened. It might help him figure out what we're dealing with."

"All right, but perhaps it's best to keep the *who* quiet. We don't need the entire North Pole talking about it, and I imagine that juicy detail would pass through Mrs. Patches to the greater metropolitan area."

I smiled. "Right. I'll keep Jack's name out of it."

"Thank you."

* * *

HAILEY, of Hailey's Holiday Treats, ran her candy business out of her home. Despite Percy's attempts to talk up the confectioner, the operation seemed pretty small at present.

"I rent kitchen space from Yuletide Yummies. I usually go to work once they close down for the day. It's a lot of late nights, but it's worth it," Hailey told us, as she showed us the assortment of wrapped goodies spread across two folding tables in her garage. "Everything stays nice and cold out here," she continued, "and then I do deliveries twice a week to make sure every order arrives fresh."

"You personally deliver everything?" I asked, quirking a brow at Corbin when Hailey wasn't looking. "That seems like a lot of extra work for you. Do any of your customers pick up their orders?"

"No," she replied, shaking her head of shoulder-length blonde hair. "I prefer to deliver everything myself. Since I work here, out of my home, it's a little too much hustle and bustle to have everyone coming and going. I have two young kids, and I just feel it would be disruptive."

"Understandable." I smiled at the witch. She was about my height and perhaps close to my age, too. I couldn't imagine having two kids yet. Sometimes I watched my niece and nephew for an entire day when Stephen had something he needed to do, and it usually took me a full day to recover afterward. I supposed I wanted my own child eventually, but the specifics still looked a little fuzzy in my mind's eye.

"I use a delivery service, Neighbor-hoot Express. Have you heard of them? It's pretty new, I think. They have carrier owls, just like at the post office. They deliver small packages all over the North Pole and suburbs. Between you and me, it's a *lot* cheaper than the postal service. I wouldn't be able to stay in business without them."

"Do you remember doing a custom order of miniature candy canes in the last week or so? They were really small, like toothpicks," I asked.

"Oh, yes. For Mr. Lowell. He's such a character, isn't he?" Hailey laughed to herself. "Is that who I can thank for the referral?"

"Something like that," Corbin replied.

"Do you have the address where those were sent?" I asked her.

Hailey hesitated, then went to a metal filing cabinet.

After a few moments, she came back to us and handed Corbin a half-sheet of paper with the order printed on it.

Peering over his shoulder, I looked at the address notes. "That's my parents' house. If the candy canes went there, surely someone would have seen them being dropped off."

"Well," Hailey interjected, "they do tend to do most of their routes at night. I don't mind, because the candies can sit out without any issue. Was there a problem with the candy canes?"

So far in our introduction and tour, I hadn't spotted any red flags that would point to Hailey herself being involved in the contamination of the candy canes. But somewhere between the candies leaving her garage and getting to my parents' house—if that was indeed where they'd been dropped off—someone else had to have gotten ahold of them.

Before I could work out the proper reply, a tawny owl swooped in, wearing a tiny blue hat with the logo for Neighbor-hoot Express embroidered on it. "Oh, hello, Larry!"

"Morning, Hailey! Do you have anything for me today? I'm on my way to the distribution center," the owl said as he perched on the back of a wooden chair.

"Oh, not yet. I'll come drop off everything this afternoon. I still have a bit of packaging to do. But thank you for asking." Hailey turned to me. "Although, while you're here," she looked back at the owl, "do you happen to know who delivered that batch of candy canes you picked up Monday afternoon?"

"Yeah, yeah, sure do. I delivered those myself!"

"Oh, you did?"

"I won't forget that journey anytime soon." Larry shuddered, his feathers ruffling at the memory. "Spooky little joint out in the woods. I'm not ashamed to say I dropped the package and flew off like my tail-feathers were on fire! I kept thinking a giant spider was going to pop out from somewhere in the trees and turn me into supper!"

My brows furrowed. "No, no that can't be right."

Larry tilted his head. "No?"

"Could you take us there?" Corbin asked.

If Hailey thought it an odd request, she didn't interject to question us.

"Do you have the time?" Larry asked.

"Erm, half past ten," Corbin said once he consulted his watch.

Larry tucked his beak, then brightened. "Yes, we'll have to hurry though. Do you have transportation?"

Corbin stepped out of the garage and spoke a word into a conjured ripple of wind. I was about to ask him what he'd done, when suddenly Ullr appeared in the sky.

"Thank you, again, Hailey," I said.

Larry blinked. "That'll do!"

Starlea was waiting near Hailey's front porch, rustling through the snow in hopes of finding a snack in her lawn. I clucked my tongue, and she gave up on her foraging. Corbin climbed onto Ullr's back while I saddled up on Starlea, and we set off, following the delivery owl out of Holiday Haven, toward the frozen woods.

9

"**W**e're nearly there!" Larry called over his wing as he began dropping his altitude. The only problem—we were on the opposite side of the fjord from the reindeer sanctuary.

Craning around, I squinted into the wind and tried to orient myself. "Are you sure this is the way, Larry? This isn't anywhere close to my parents' property."

"Yep, yep. I'm sure!" the owl hooted, dropping even lower. "There is it!"

Twisting back around to face forward, I pulled Starlea to the right in order to see past Corbin and Ullr. Ahead of us, the thick trees parted to form a small clearing, and a twisting snake of smoke floated up from a small, round cottage.

"It's not so scary in the daytime," Larry added, "but at night? Whew! No thank you!"

I wasn't even sure how the owl had managed to find the tiny cottage in the first place, let alone while he was supposed to be going to my parents' farmhouse. We were miles off track, over the fjord, and deep into the frozen woods.

"Apparently you get what you pay for," I muttered to myself. "I should probably tell Hailey to go with the official postal service for out-of-town deliveries."

Larry beat his wings a few times to hover in place. "Need anything else? I should be going soon," the owl said. "I need to get to the distribution center before noon."

"Thank you, Larry," I said as Corbin pulled Ullr into a holding pattern. I drew up on Starlea's reins to slow her down. "One more thing, when you left the candy, did you see anyone take it?"

"No, like I said before, I shot out of here like confetti from a cannon!"

I smiled. The owl had a knack for colorful phrases. "Right. Well, thanks again."

"Anytime! And remember, if you need anything delivered, you can trust the Neighbor-hoot Express!"

"Yeah ... trust they'll lose your package in the middle of the woods," I said once he was gone.

"No kidding," Corbin said before urging Ullr down to the ground. "Where are we? I've never been this deep in the woods before."

"Neither have I," I said, which was really quite a statement. I loved spending my free afternoons—rare though they might be—out exploring the woods and back acreage of my parents' property. The sanctuary's grounds ended at the water though; there was no question this cottage was on its own land.

The question was whose land. Well, that and what any of this had to do with the pixies.

We touched down in the clearing and a strange feeling washed over me. I could understand what had made the owl so skittish about the place. There was a certain eeriness clinging to the air. Or maybe it was the absolute silence that gave me pause. There were no birds chirping in the surrounding trees. No wind rustling through the evergreens. It was almost like something supernatural was blocking out any sound. Starlea could sense it, too. The thick hairs along her neck stood on end.

"Should we knock?" I asked, my tone hushed as I gave my reindeer a reassuring pat.

"I guess so," Corbin replied, dismounting beside me. He kept one hand wrapped around Ullr's reins and I wondered if the winged horse was prone to spooking. The last thing either of us needed was to get stranded out here.

I drew in a breath and approached the cottage's front door. It was a small abode, even smaller than my groundskeeper quarters back at the sanctuary, and that was saying something. The window shades were all drawn, making it impossible to see inside. But the smoke pouring from the chimney was a good indication that someone was home.

Gingerly, I rapped my knuckles against the door three times, then took a large step backward. As I waited, I noticed there were footprints in the snow going to and from a pile of covered firewood near the tree line. The prints were small, most likely belonging to a petite female or a child. Some of the tension in my chest eased.

The front door of the hut remained closed, but an eyeball peered out at me through the front window before disappearing again as soon as it saw me notice it. "Um, hello?" I called out, knocking softly again. "My name is Lumi Northrop, I'm from the North Star Reindeer Sanctuary."

I'd found that using my full title could go a long ways toward garnering a stranger's trust. My family was well known throughout the Pole and smaller havens. Surely whoever lived here would have heard of my family before.

Corbin came to stand beside me. "And I am Prince Corbin Frost," he added, before sliding me a sidelong glance.

I shrugged. Out of the corner of my eye, I noticed Ullr's nose was pressed to the ground near the hut. He used one hoof to shuffle some of the snow out of the way, and a shock of red caught my eye. "Corbin, look! There's candy cane pieces in the snow."

Corbin followed my finger and realized what his horse was up to. "Whoa, there. You're trouble enough without the help of that stuff," he told his steed as he kicked snow over the crushed bits of candy and stomped it down just for good measure.

Ullr snorted and continued to rake at the ground with his powerful hoof. Starlea came over to join the horse's investigation.

Corbin sighed and reached into his pocket. He produced an oat ball and held it up to get their attention. "Promise you'll leave those alone, and I'll give you this one now, and another when we head back home. All right?"

Ullr whinnied in agreement and Corbin extended the treat toward his mouth, then pulled out a second for Starlea.

"I guess at least we know this is the place," I said, knocking softly again. Ullr finished his treat and went back to his treasure hunt in the snow. He overturned more broken shards of candy cane. "Uh, Corbin."

Corbin shot his horse the look of a disappointed father as he started to kick more snow over the new pile of candy. "Wait," he said, pausing his efforts. "Look, Lumi, there's a whole trail of them here!"

There was no sign that anyone was going to open the door for us. With a sigh, I stepped off the small wooden step and caught up to Corbin and Ullr as they followed the trail of broken peppermint shards around the side of the house. We made it across the untouched snowbank at the rear of the house and stepped into the tree canopy when a burst of magic snapped through the air and hit the tree a few feet to the left of Corbin. A loud *crack* echoed through the preternaturally quiet wood, and the top half of the tree toppled over. Starlea leaped into the air while Ullr spooked and kicked his back legs.

"Stop right there!" a cold voice commanded. "One more step and the next spell has your name on it."

Slowly, we turned around and found ourselves faced off with a slight woman, a good four inches shorter than me and much thinner. Judging by the deep lines in her face she was rather old and had lived a hard life. Purple magic pulsed in her hand, proving her warning to be true.

"I don't know what you think you're doing here, but this land is not for you," she said, taking a series of steps closer to us.

I held up my hands in surrender. "Please, we're not here to hurt you or anyone else. We're trying to save the frost pixies and we think the answer might be in these woods."

I quickly explained what had happened to the pixies, and showed her the trail of peppermint in the snow. "Please, we only want to find out the truth about what happened to the pixies and how we can restore them."

When I finished, the witch spoke, the magic still floating in her hand. "You might be the guardian of the reindeer, Lumi Northrop, but *I* am the guardian of these woods and their inhabitants," she said, squaring her narrow shoulders. "I had nothing to do with what has happened to the frost pixies."

"But it looks like they might not be the only ones in danger." I gestured once more at the peppermint in the snow. "Who else lives in these woods?"

The witch's expression shifted and with a flick of her hand, the magic vanished in a puff of purple smoke. She hiked up her skirt and bustled into the woods, passing us without a word.

Corbin and I exchanged a silent glance, neither of us seeming to know what to do. Corbin tied Ullr's reins to the tree beside the demolished one and we hurried after the witch. We'd come this far. We couldn't go home empty-handed now.

Of course, I wasn't crazy about the idea of going home in pieces either.

"What is the meaning of this?" the witch's voice cut through the woods and both Corbin and I picked up our pace. We ran ahead and found the witch standing before a huge tree, its trunk so wide that even if Corbin and I were to stand on opposite sides and wrap our arms around it, we wouldn't have been able to touch one another's fingers.

Tiny glittering eyes peered down from the myriad of branches.

"Wood sprites!" Corbin whispered. "A whole colony of them."

The sprites were something of a mix between walking sticks and fairies. They were no bigger than my hand, their limbs twisted and gnarled like branches, while their wings were light green, transparent but for thin reedy veins.

At the base of the tree, an assortment of items lay scattered, with shards of peppermint scattered throughout. Old books, a metal scale, a stone mortar and pestle, a large, scorched metal bucket.

"Oh, you nasty little beasties!" the witch howled as she sprang into action to gather her belongings. "Making me think I was going half out of my gourd over losing everything!" She scoffed and snatched up the spell-casting book. Her face blanched when she saw the page it was open to. "You've been casting magic? Tell me, what have you done?"

"Nothing they didn't deserve!" one of the sprites exclaimed, shaking a tiny fist.

The witch snapped the book shut and clutched it to her chest as she turned toward me. "I'm afraid you were right. Someone did tamper with those candies. This is a mischief spell, but it's made for much larger bodies. If applied to the pixies, well, it would make them go—"

"Full gremlins after midnight?" Corbin interjected.

The witch didn't look like the sort to be up to date on

her '80s cult classics and the reference flew over her head. Too busy scolding the wood sprites, she didn't even really seem to notice. "Why did you do this? What did the pixies ever do to you?"

"They called us ugly!" a sprite called back.

A hiss went up among the collective.

"The pixies and fairies are always the ones who get asked to perform for special events. No one ever thinks of us! All we wanted was to dance alongside them, but they told us we were too *ugly* to dance. That no one would want to see a bunch of flying sticks!"

"Sticks!" another one called out among a chorus of jeers.

"Sticks with wings!"

The witch huffed and turned away, disgusted. "Come, child. I will help you set this right."

The sprites hissed and booed as we helped the witch gather her belongings. "I grant them a *drop* of magic and this is how they repay me," she fumed as she led the way into her cottage.

The interior was sparse, with threadbare rugs and shabby furnishings. A cauldron sat in the fireplace. As I approached it, I expected some magical concoction but instead found a hearty stew simmering.

"I never should have trusted them with power," the witch said, shaking her head as she went into the small kitchen and began rustling through the cabinets. A rustic worktable sat in the middle, covered with herbs and small unmarked bottles. "They begged me for decades," she continued, "and I only gave in because I thought it would keep them safe. This world is a changed place. I wanted them to be able to protect themselves, should they ever need it."

The witch worked with her long, gnarled fingers. She moved so quickly and with experienced movements. It was like watching a gourmet chef cook. She didn't need a grimoire or a recipe; everything was by feel, sight, smell. I kept my distance out of respect, but couldn't keep my eyes off of her.

When she finally looked up at me, her pupils were wide and filled with light. "I am sorry for what they have done to the pixies."

"It's not your fault," I told her. "It sounds like you were just trying to help them."

The witch scoffed, but didn't try to argue.

"If that darn owl hadn't gotten off course and dropped the candies here in the first place, maybe none of this would have happened," I continued, still working it all together in my own head.

"Oh, I don't know about that," the witch said, bustling around the worktable, a small amber-colored glass bottle in one hand. "They're opportunistic and sneaky. I imagine some other circumstance would have come along for them to get their revenge."

"Here, Lumi. Take this." She pressed the bottle into my hands. "There's a dropper inside. One drop per pixie is all it should take to reverse the spell."

"Thank you, um, you still haven't told me your name."

The witch frowned as she gave me a long appraising look. Finally, she softened and spoke, "You may call me Opal."

"Thank you, Opal." I smiled warmly at the witch and

rose to my feet. "If you ever need anything, please come to the sanctuary. Any time."

She inclined her head toward me.

"The Frost Kingdom owes you a debt, as well," Corbin added. "Our aid is at your disposal should you ever have need of it."

Opal followed us to the door and softly closed it after us without another word.

"Come on," I said, carefully wrapping the bottle in a handkerchief before placing it inside my coat pocket, "let's get to Doc Patches."

10

"We're so sorry, Lumi."

"I know, Astrid." I smiled. "You've already told me at least a dozen times since yesterday."

The pixie beat her wings together, sending a shower of snowflakes to the ground below her tiny feet. "Do you forgive us, then?"

"There's nothing to forgive. You were under the influence of some pretty powerful magic. I don't blame any of you for what happened."

Astrid glanced over her shoulder, up toward the main house. "I don't get the feeling your mother feels the same way."

I cringed. "Yeah … I think she's still a little mad about the whole reindeer droppings on her cashmere sweater incident. She'll come around though, you'll see. Just give her some time."

"Understood." Astrid nodded, though she still looked a little crestfallen. I made a mental note to speak with my mom about it. It would be best for everyone if we could move forward and put the whole messy situation in the past.

"In any case, I'm just glad you're back," I told the pixie as I adjusted my scarf. "What's going on with the performance for the solstice? It's only a few days away. Did Pandora decide what to do?"

Astrid's smile rebounded. "She's letting us perform."

"That's good. Although I imagine Pia and her Poinsettia Performers were none too pleased."

Even though it turned out Pia had nothing to do with the poisoned candy canes, she still rubbed me the wrong way, and it was hard to feel too sorry for her.

Astrid got a gleam in her eye and moved her hand over her mouth, indicating it was sealed closed.

I laughed and got up from my seat on the stack of hay bales. "I should get back to work. There's still a lot to do around here, and then I have to go into town to see Aunt Viv. Mom talked her into making a dress for me."

"A dress? But the summer solstice party isn't really for dresses, Lumi. Didn't anyone tell you? It's all about sand and sun!"

"Oh, I know. This is for the publicity stop on Jack's tour. She's agreed to host it here at the barn."

"A royal event, right here?" Astrid exclaimed, flying a little higher before bursting into a spin that sent another burst of snowflakes into the air.

"It's not for a few weeks, but yes, it's going to be quite a sight. Mom said the royal party planner has a near endless budget. Last thing I overheard, they were talking about creating a frozen dance floor suspended over the field, with a live band, and seals that could balance trays of appetizers on their noses."

Astrid giggled. "Oh my!"

"Yeah." I shook my head. "I told Dad he needs to keep her feet on the ground before she runs off to be a full-time royal party planner. Corbin's so nice he'd probably give her the job if she asked."

"And what about you, Lumi? Do you think you'll be running away to Frost Castle anytime soon?" Astrid clasped her hands together under her chin. "You would make for a lovely princess!"

"I'm taking everything one day at a time," I told the pixie. "I don't think either Corbin or I is in a race to the altar. Besides, I think for the time being, Corbin is focused on getting Jack married off before he starts thinking about it for himself. There's a certain order to these things when it comes to the royal family."

Astrid tried not to look disappointed, but her wings sagged as she dropped her hands back to her sides. "I suppose that's true."

I crossed the barn and grabbed the handles of the wheelbarrow. As I rolled it toward the farthest stall, Astrid buzzed back over my shoulder. "Lumi, at least promise me that I'll get to be the flower girl when you marry the prince! It's all I've ever wanted!"

I laughed softly. "All you've ever wanted?" I teased. "Corbin only came into my life six months ago, Astrid."

The pixie tossed up her hands. "Well, I just mean, whenever you get married. I've always wanted to be a part of it, somehow."

"I see." My heart warmed and I gave the pixie my

solemn oath, "Well, in that case, yes. I promise you can be my flower girl."

"Yippee!" The pixie shot to the rafters and swirled around, until it looked like the aftermath of a fireworks display, with the glittering blue and silver snowflakes floating down gently to the floor.

WALKING into the summer solstice celebration looked a little different than I'd expected, considering I had not one, but two, Frost men to escort me inside the beach bubble. By way of an apology for their fight in the Holiday Haven town square, Corbin asked Jack if he wanted to attend the party with us. It didn't take much convincing to get him to go along with it, once he heard there would be ladies in skimpy swimsuits.

"This is wild!" I exclaimed, marveling at the interior of the large dome. The air was balmy and a slight breeze wafted through the palm trees, rustling the coconuts nestled among the fronds. I'd never seen the ocean before in person, but the scene inside the bubble looked just like a postcard photo of a tropical seascape. Gentle waves lapped at the white sand, nipping at the ankles of the people playing at the water's edge. A volleyball net was set up and a half a dozen people were playing a game for a crowd of onlookers. Children ran and played in the surf, while others built sandcastles under large striped umbrellas while their parents looked on.

A tiki bar with a thatched roof looked like one of the most popular spots, with dozens of people enjoying colorful drinks. I smiled at Clarence, who was working the busy bar, decked out in a Hawaiian-print shirt and a wide-brim straw hat.

We were escorted to a cluster of striped tents where we could slough off our winter gear and change into our summer attire.

"Looking good, Lumi!" Jack told me as I reemerged from my tent a few minutes later.

Corbin elbowed him in the ribs. "Keep your eyes in your head. Don't make me regret inviting you to this thing."

Jack sighed dramatically. "What, I can't even compliment the woman? Yeesh, Corbin. Green is *not* your color."

Corbin started to reply, but I caught his arm and looped mine through it. "It's okay. I think we all look pretty good."

"Thank you, Lumi," Jack replied, preening a little to better showcase his bared torso and bright red swim trunks.

Both Frost brothers were in good shape. Corbin's beachwear was a little more reserved than his brother's, opting for a tank top in addition to his board shorts. Secretly, I thought Corbin's physique was even more impressive than Jack's. Eat your heart out, ladies of the North Pole.

As we ventured farther into the bubble, Jack snagged an entire tray of fruity drinks from a passing server, barely taking his eyes away from the activity. "Are those *mermaids*?" he asked, his eyes going wide. "Mermaid lifeguards. Why haven't we come to this party before? Oh, look, that redheaded one is waving at me. I think perhaps I need to go for a swim."

With a waggle of his brows, he started to walk away, but Corbin reached out and snagged his brother by the arm. "Behave yourself, Jack. The last thing we need is pictures of you canoodling with a mermaid all over the tabloids tomorrow morning."

Jack scoffed. "Oh, come on. I promise to keep it PG … thirteen."

"Jack—"

It was too late. He was already running into the surf, likely to pretend to drown in hopes of getting CPR.

"Just let him go," I said with a giggle. "Mermaids are pretty feisty. I don't think they'll put up with his antics for too long."

"I shouldn't have told him about the party," Corbin muttered, shaking his head. "I actually wanted this to be a special night, just you and me—"

He paused and met my eyes, his own wide as if he'd slipped and said something he hadn't meant to.

"It is special," I assured him. "I always feel special when I'm with you."

He smiled and cupped the side of my face. "I'm glad to hear you say that. There's something I've been wanting to tell you for a long time now." He paused and cleared his throat. "Lumi, I know we haven't been together all that long, and our time together has had its challenges … but I hope you know how much you mean to me. I've—well, Lumi, I've fallen hopelessly in love with you."

Tears sprang to my eyes as I nodded and collapsed into his arms. "I love you, too, Corbin."

We kissed under the magical sunset and I knew that with Corbin by my side, every day would feel like a holiday.

When we parted, I took his hand and dragged my gaze to the tiki bar. "Now, what do you say we go get one of those frozen drinks with a little umbrella in it?"

"I'm right behind you!" Corbin said.

And I knew that he always would be.

THANK you for reading Peppermint Pixies. I hope you enjoyed reading this continuation of Lumi and Corbin's story. If you are new to my work, a great place to go from here is my boxed set for my longest (and now completed) Beechwood Harbor Magic Mysteries series. You can get this boxed set for free with Kindle Unlimited or buy it for the special price of $0.99.

Also, be sure to check out the other books in the Winter Witches of Holiday Haven world! Find them on Amazon or you can see all of the books here: www.WinterWitchesBooks.com

If you're in the mood for more Christmas stories, I have two festive novellas available:

A Very Beechwood Christmas — A Beechwood Harbor Magic Mystery novella

Grimoires and Gingerbread — A Sugar Shack Witch Mystery novella

SIGN up for my newsletter to make sure you're the first to know when I have a new release, promotion, or fun freebies! You get two prequels just for joining, so head over to my website to get signed up now. www.DanielleGarrettBooks.com/newsletter

IF YOU'D LIKE to connect with other readers, come join the Bat Wings Book Club on Facebook. It's my happy little corner of the internet and I love chatting with readers and sharing behind the scenes fun.

UNTIL NEXT TIME, **happy reading!**
  Danielle Garrett
  www.DanielleGarrettBooks.com

**One town. Two spunky leading ladies.
More magic than you can shake a wand at.
Welcome to Beechwood Harbor.**

*Come join the fun in Beechwood Harbor, the little town where witches,
shifters, ghosts, and vamps all live, work, play, and—mostly—get
along!*

The two main series set in this world are the Beechwood Harbor
Magic Mysteries and the Beechwood Harbor Ghost Mysteries.

In the following pages you will find more information about
those books, as well as my other works available.

Alternatively, you can find a complete reading list on my website:

www.DanielleGarrettBooks.com

ABOUT THE AUTHOR

As a lifelong bookworm, Danielle Garrett has always loved dreaming of fantastic places and the stories they have to share. Through her love of reading, she's followed along on hundreds of adventures through the eyes of wizards, princesses, elves, and some rather wonderful everyday people as well. This lifelong passion led her into the world of writing and she has now achieved the dream she's held since the second grade and become an author herself.

Danielle lives in Oregon, and while she travels as often as possible, she wouldn't call anywhere else home. She shares her life with her husband and their house full of animals. When she's not writing, she can be found serving as the dedicated servant to three extremely spoiled cats or chasing down the most recent item the puppy has turned into a chew toy.

Visit Danielle today at her website or say "hello" on Facebook.

www.DanielleGarrettBooks.com

Printed in the USA
CPSIA information can be obtained
at www.ICGtesting.com
LVHW050258030924
789900LV00032B/405

9 798535 271996